His gaze locked with hers. 'I'd rather tell you that I have enjoyed the last four months with you more than any I can remember.'

Georgia's eyebrows rose in disbelief. 'Sure,' she said. 'It must have been a hoot for you. You've enjoyed being woken up by a colicky baby ten times a night, and having a grumpy, sleep-deprived flatmate to live with.' Why on earth would he?

'Absolutely.' The tilt of his lips confirmed that he had only pleasant memories, and though he spoke quietly his tone of voice sounded the truth. 'I became acquainted with Elsa, and she's gorgeous—like her mother.'

Georgia tilted her head. 'Same temperament, you mean?'

Max nodded. 'She's determined and independent, yes.'

They were teasing each other, and she was beginning to enjoy it too much. This was far too dangerous for her peace of mind, and she tried to steer the topic away into more general waters. Maybe he did have an agenda with her after all—or he'd managed to beam in on one of her fantasies.

'It is a glorious night,' she said.

Max wouldn't be diverted. 'I've appreciated each and every vision of you at night since Elsa was born.'

A mother to five sons, **Fiona McArthur** is an Australian midwife who loves to write. Medical™ Romance gives Fiona the scope to write about all the wonderful aspects of adventure, romance, medicine and midwifery that she feels so passionate about—as well as an excuse to travel! So now that the boys are older, her husband Ian and youngest son Rory are off with Fiona to meet new people, see new places, and have wonderful adventures. Fiona's website is at www.fionamcarthur.com

Recent titles by the same author:

THEIR SPECIAL-CARE BABY
THE SURGEON'S SPECIAL GIFT
THE DOCTOR'S SURPRISE BRIDE
DANGEROUS ASSIGNMENT
THE PREGNANT MIDWIFE

THE
MIDWIFE'S BABY

BY
FIONA McARTHUR

MILLS & BOON®
Pure reading pleasure

First published in Great Britain 2008
Harlequin Mills & Boon Limited,
Eton House, 18-24 Paradise Road, Richmond, Surrey TW9 1SR

© Fiona McArthur 2008

ISBN: 978 0 263 19893 5

Set in Times Roman 10¾ on 12¼ pt
15-0408-41019

Printed and bound in Great Britain
by Antony Rowe Ltd, Chippenham, Wiltshire

THE
MIDWIFE'S BABY

TO THE MAYTONE GIRLS, FRIENDS INDEED,
WHO INSPIRE ME.

CHAPTER ONE

THE chapel floated like a snowflake against the backdrop of the lush Hunter Valley Gardens and the string quartet drifted silvery notes out over the waiting guests.

Max Beresford stood tall and straight at the front of the church and realised that despite the romantic venue he'd condemned himself to the type of loveless marriage his parents had.

Give me a sign, God. Am I a fool for going through with this?

The procession music started. Too late.

Max tilted his chin slightly as he watched the matron of honour walk haltingly towards him in some screechingly fashionable apricot material.

There was something about the dogged yet vulnerable expression on the woman's face that aroused his sympathy because he'd approached the altar with just such a halting advance.

Max frowned. Was there a problem or was his new cousin-in-law-to-be unbearably nervous?

Embarrassed didn't make sense because she looked gorgeous—fertile with her baby bump bulging beneath the shiny fabric—but gorgeous nonetheless.

She paused again and seemed to suck air in through gritted teeth before she raised her chin and resumed her approach.

Max knew Tayla had been reluctant to include her midwife cousin, Georgia, in the wedding party but he'd thought that had been because of Georgia's unfashionable pregnancy and some vague hint that she was depressed. Maybe there were other reasons.

Before he could ruminate on that thought his non-blushing bride staged her spectacular entry and the gasps from the congregation drew Max's eyes towards his future wife.

Max could do nothing but stare as feathers rippled and parted in the breeze and held him spellbound.

He blinked in disbelief. Tayla seemed to have been devoured by a white duck.

Framed against the door for an extended moment, his bride's shapely arms and legs stretched from beneath a strapless froth of feathers that only just covered her thighs at the front and fell in a frothy tail to the floor at the back.

A large apricot bow around her tiny waist matched the rose in her father's lapel.

Good grief, Max thought, and suppressed a smile. He'd fallen into *Swan Lake* and he had never felt less like a prince.

His bride floated up beside him, as did one of the feathers that had come unstuck and drifted just ahead of her in an eddy, and went to hand her feathered fan to the matron of honour.

Cousin Georgia was not having a good day as she missed the one cue she'd been assigned. He could see Tayla remained seriously unimpressed with her attendant.

For Georgia Winton, being matron of honour had assumed the nightmare proportions she had hoped it wouldn't.

The first unexpected labour contraction had hit her as she'd entered the church at the precise moment the whole congregation had noticed her entrance.

The next contraction had grown to such intensity she almost dropped the bouquet as her cousin handed it to her.

When she was able to, Georgia offered an apologetic glance at the bride and groom, which neither acknowledged. Tayla had tossed her head in disgust and Max had continued to stare, bemused, at Tayla's dress.

Georgia clutched the bouquet like the dead duck it resembled and forced her shoulders to drop as the pain eased away. Distraction, distraction, distraction, she reminded herself. There was plenty of that.

Max Beresford, the groom, was pretty distracting. She'd known of him, but until now not by sight as he'd missed rehearsals because of some crisis at the hospital.

The real Max was tall, broad-shouldered and far too handsome for his own good, but his kind eyes had surprised her with their warmth.

Though younger than she'd expected, he looked every inch the new department head of obstetrics for the North Coast Region of Hospitals—a position he was taking up after Tayla's and his honeymoon—and she was surprised how much she instinctively felt that Tayla had chosen well.

After her baby was born, Max would apparently find her a midwife's position in the region, so she really did hope she wouldn't ruin his wedding.

Max's brother, Paul, who had played groom each time they'd practised the wedding service, seemed pleasant enough but not a warm person and he stood beside Max now as a paler shade of his brother.

Unfortunately Paul's eyes were fixed a little too intently on his brother's wife-to-be.

Meanwhile Tayla, gloriously aware of everyone's attention, proceeded to lift her eyes theatrically towards the stained-glass window and shimmy her feathers.

Georgia could see no softness or devotion or anything redeeming from her cousin despite the perfect setting and the man beside her. Though she had adamantly said to Georgia that of course she loved Max.

On the groom's part, even the smile Max gave his fiancée seemed strained and disconnected.

Georgia ached with disappointment. Weddings shouldn't be like this. What was wrong with everybody? Except for her parents, who had remained blissfully in love until their deaths, she had begun to despair that all marriages were destined to be travesties.

Tayla she could understand. Tayla had always wanted the extravagant white wedding and the rich husband, topped off by the bridal magazine shoot currently in progress.

While her cousin would enjoy being married to a handsome consultant as she flew in to join Max briefly for social occasions in whatever city or town he visited, Tayla didn't intend that her marriage would markedly change her life.

A tiny worry line drew Max's thick black brows together even further and Georgia glared at him for not savouring the moment. Didn't he realise the sacredness of marriage?

What was in it for Max if he didn't have some affection for his bride?

Romantically, Georgia had hoped this wedding would restore her faith in true love. She'd hoped there would be a incandescent joy between these two as they stood before God and declared their troth.

Then the third contraction gripped her belly and all else was forgotten as the searing pain snatched her breath at the peak. This time the intensity drew a stifled gasp she couldn't contain. Even the minister looked across at her with raised eyebrows.

It wasn't fair. Labour was supposed to start with gentle regular contractions, gradually increasing in intensity. She should have been supported by her midwife friends at home, with birdsong playing. Not the Wedding March.

The only thing bird-like about these pains were that they flew straight to a pain score of ten.

When the contraction finally eased she accepted that it was likely the wedding would go on without her.

Georgia chewed her bottom lip and tried to focus on the glorious blue-green stained-glass window until the minister began to speak again. In the lull before the next pain, she could almost believe she could wait at least until the man-and-wife part of the service.

Tayla was going to kill her and when she looked at the bride she wanted to cry. Pregnancy hormones, of course—but, then Tayla had always made her want to cry.

She tried to concentrate on the ballet of the shooting fountains in the artificial lake below— surely the next contraction would be further apart— until a tiny clicking pop sent the trickle of warm fluid down her leg and forced her to call it a day.

'Excuse me,' she whispered to the minister as she edged away from the altar towards the side door of the church.

'You're not going anywhere,' Tayla hissed, but this time Georgia didn't hear.

Please, God, she prayed silently, don't let anyone notice the tiny rivulets of fluid in her wake. She could feel the eyes of the congregation on her back.

Suddenly the trickle became a gush and her baby kicked and squirmed in an agitated dance that evicted any thought of who was watching and sent prickles of unease down Georgia's spine.

This didn't feel right and her baby's panic was communicated to Georgia even though she had never experienced labour before. At work she'd seen labour go wrong and she tried not to allow those memories to intrude.

She remembered the words of her Calmbirth midwife—listen to your body. Listen to your instincts. Her belly heaved as her baby twisted again. Her instinct said she needed to go to the hospital and her baby demanded speed.

She lifted her eyes in panic. She needed help, and suddenly help was there. The steady gaze of Max grounded her panic with calmness and a strong, reassuring hand on her shoulder.

She swallowed the lump of fear in her throat. The last time she'd seen him he'd been at the altar with Tayla. She darted a look to the front of the church and her cousin glared with real menace towards both of them.

'Your waters have broken?'

She nodded, still stunned that Max had left his bride. Georgia didn't have the mental space to go there. Tayla would have to get used to being married to a doctor, but not yet—at least not until after the wedding.

'You've been having contractions.' His voice was

gentle and she looked back at him because it was better than looking at the gaping assembly.

Her baby twisted and turned like a fish on a hook and she cupped her stomach and grabbed his hand as the next contraction squeezed.

'Hard and fast. Something's wrong.' It was difficult to get the words out through the pain. 'Something else came out with the water. I'm thinking cord prolapse.'

Cord prolapse was one of the true obstetric emergencies and they both knew it.

If a baby hadn't 'dropped' or engaged its head in the pelvis, a loop of cord could fall between the baby's head and the bottom of the uterus when the waters broke. With four weeks to go in Georgia's pregnancy her baby hadn't dropped yet so it was dreadfully possible.

Any contractions she had after that could force the hard head of the baby onto the presenting cord and cut off the flow of oxygen from mother to baby. With no oxygen her baby would die.

If that was the case they needed to try to keep Georgia's baby's head from coming down onto the umbilical cord. Minutes counted.

'I'm scared, Max.' She'd never met this man in her life and suddenly it felt OK to call him Max.

His eyes softened and he nodded once. 'I know. We need to get you to the hospital ASAP.'

He flipped open his phone and spoke briefly into it. 'Let's get you outside to the car. An ambulance can meet us on the road if we don't beat them there.'

He scooped her up in his arms and she cringed. 'Your beautiful suit.'

'It's only a suit.' He grinned down at her and incredibly his eyes were golden and caring and she suddenly felt her baby had a chance, even though the odds were stacked against them.

Another contraction coiled viciously through her and she moaned. This was terrifying.

Max carried her swiftly to his black limousine. White ribbons fluttered on the long bonnet and the JUST MARRIED placard sat proudly on the boot.

Georgia shifted in his arms as she twisted her neck to see. 'Not this car, Max. The seats.'

'To hell with the seats. At least we have room and the windows are tinted.'

Max's chauffeur's usually impassive expression faltered as Max deposited the wrong woman in the wedding car.

'Newcastle Hospital ASAP. I'll pay the speeding fines,' Max said over his shoulder as he climbed in after her. He pulled shut the door before he sat opposite Georgia and shrugged out of his jacket.

The car accelerated away from the kerb and Georgia fell back in a heap. Max leaned across from the facing seat to help her balance.

'Can you check and tell me if you can feel the umbilical cord?' He smiled sympathetically at her and suddenly it was OK. They were a team working together to help save a baby—her baby.

With difficulty she knelt on the soft leather seat, closed her eyes mortified as a rivulet of pink fluid disappeared down the back of the seat, and hitched up the wet satin creation designed by a leading Sydney fashion house.

That morning, when she'd struggled with clipping her thigh-high stockings to the garter belt, she'd thought it a shame no one would see the pretty lace of the belt. What a joke. Once she got to the hospital, everyone would be looking at her.

As she slipped her hand down into her panties she knew what she would find—she could feel it beating like her own heartbeat except slower. Sure enough, a loop of umbilical cord fell into her hand.

Before she could confirm her finding to Max, the next contraction was on top of her and with this pain the urge to push was overpowering. It couldn't happen this quick! They were supposed to stop the labour until they could get her to operating theatre and do a Caesarean section to save her baby.

'Ma-ax,' she wailed and she grabbed his hand, put her chin on her chest and pushed, unable to stop herself.

Still calm, his voice was kind. 'There's no time for modesty. You know that, don't you, Georgia? Let me see.'

Max's face was composed but in that moment she saw the stressed beat of the vein in his temple and she knew he doubted her baby's chances despite his calm voice.

The look of surprise on his face made a tiny shaft of hope slice through the pain to imprint on Georgia's thoughts.

'First baby?' His eyes met hers in question.

'Absolutely. Probably last,' she gasped.

He smiled at that and sat back. 'Well, your baby is ready to come and is almost here. Let nature finish the job, Georgia.'

That was all she needed to find the rest of her strength and with the next pain fast on the heels of the last she concentrated from deep within herself and willed her baby to fly out into the world before the lack of oxygen from the compression of the cord could take away her life.

When she opened her eyes Max was unwinding the cord from around the baby's neck and lifting her towards Georgia, and incredibly a miniature angry red face screwed up to emit a bellow that almost lifted the roof off the car.

Max laughed and she blinked and looked again at this tiny roaring child of immense determination and began to shake in shock.

'My God.' Max wiped his eyes on his upper arm and then grabbed his suit jacket and rubbed her baby dry before he leant forward to slip the bodice strap off Georgia's shoulder to allow one side of her dress to fall to expose her skin. 'Here, keep her warm.'

Still chuckling, he placed the baby against Georgia's bare skin, flipped the jacket over to the dry side and tucked it around them both.

'Congratulations,' he said, and shook his head in disbelief. 'I'm afraid her father missed her arrival.'

Georgia shuddered. 'We didn't miss him.' Her

baby was still slightly wet and slippery and still roaring her head off and Georgia soothed her little round head that hadn't even had time to change shape for the journey through her pelvis.

'Poor baby.' She ducked her head and kissed her downy cheek. 'Do you have a headache from your quick trip?'

Max listened to the soft maternal whispers from a woman he barely knew and felt incredibly touched by a scene he'd seen so many times in so many circumstances—but never like this.

'I think you might be right about her headache.' Max shook his head again and the smile on his face felt bigger than any he'd had in the last few years. This birth brought back the notion that there could still be immense satisfaction in his chosen profession.

He'd known he needed to get back to the grass roots of it all and away from the consultancy, and board meetings, the constant demand for more high-tech medical apparatus and the financial headaches and heartaches that being head of the obstetric department left him with.

This new position promised exposure to the real world of obstetrics again. While a percentage of his duties would remain administrative, there was an expectation he would work in each hospital to gain insight into the obstetric viability of each facility.

If he was honest, that was the carrot that had got him into this marriage mess in the first place. This moment in time had proved how much more rewarding hands-on obstetrics was for him but he'd have time to think of that later.

Georgia's baby finally quietened and after a quick glance to ensure all was well he suggested to his driver that he slow the car to a reasonable pace as they finished the forty-minute drive to the hospital.

This Georgia, she was something special to have come through this with a calmness and serenity that should have been shattered, especially as, being a midwife, she'd known the complications that could ensue.

Unexpectedly the loud sound of rhythmic sucking could be heard and Max felt the smile widen on his face again.

'Umm. Isn't breastfeeding supposed to be noise-less or does this child of yours do everything spec-tacularly and with high volume?'

'I think she's loud. I should call her Thor—or Thoreen.'

'Speaking of "thor", are you?'

'Very funny.' She shook her head at him and for the first time in many years he felt like a child rebuked by an adult and his lips twitched.

She got over it quickly, though. 'Now you mention it, what are we going to do with the disaster down here ruining your upholstery? I don't suppose you have two cord clamps and a pair of scissors?'

He stripped off his elegant neckpiece. 'I do have a cord tie.'

She giggled and then covered her mouth. 'I'm

sorry. I'm feeling light-headed with relief and I'm being silly.'

He pulled a snowy white teatowel from the bottle compartment and folded it. 'Pop this between your legs.' He handed the towel to her. 'Let's just settle for that one knot in the cord with the tie and we'll bundle it all up still connected and they can sort it out at the hospital. Are you bleeding?'

She shook her head. 'Not since she started to feed.'

He marvelled at the wonders of nature without the usual drugs given at the end of labour. 'Thor looks about five pounds. How early is she by your dates?'

'Four weeks and two days.' He'd hazard a guess she was counting days from conception.

'Did ultrasounds confirm those dates?'

She lifted her chin at him. 'Ever the doctor. Why do so many obstetricians think ultrasounds know more than the mother?'

He chuckled at that. 'True. Sometimes ultrasounds can cloud issues that don't need clouding. And other times an ultrasound can clarify things.'

'Hmmph,' Georgia said. 'You can't beat good clinical skills. Technology is one of the things I won't get bogged down in when I start to practise again.'

He couldn't remember the last time he'd heard someone hmmph. 'We won't get into that discussion or maybe we'll save it till later.'

'And my baby's name is not Thor.'

'Wowser.' He settled back into the seat as all the chores that could be done had been done. The rest could wait.

He was a mess and her dress had seen better days too. His shirt was unbuttoned at the neck from when he'd pulled his tie off. The long sleeves had been hiked unevenly up to his elbows and he cupped his hands on one knee and decided he'd definitely have to throw out the suit.

He looked across at her. Actually, she looked pretty good. 'So what are you going to call her?'

She laughed at that and he loved the way she threw her whole face into the laugh. No attempt to save on laughter lines and she did have a lot to be thankful for.

'What do you call a child that arrived like this and roared so vigorously at birth?' She looked down at the now content baby. 'I could call her Maxine.'

She was delightful and with a thud he remembered he was almost married. 'That would really set the cat among the pigeons,' he drawled.

He saw the moment she remembered Tayla. 'Oh, my God. Your wedding. I'm so sorry.'

'Later. It will be a drama in due time. No use thinking about it now.'

CHAPTER TWO

TAYLA'S wild eyes were slitted shafts of fury in her narrow face as she stormed into Georgia's hospital room. Anger vibrated off her in waves and even the baby stirred in her sleep with the malevolence emanating from Tayla.

Max thought it all lost a little credibility with the feathers.

Normally Tayla was a very attractive woman but in this instance he decided he might have had a lucky escape. He stayed motionless, leaning up against the wall with his arms crossed, and waited for his fiancée to see her cousin was not alone.

Tayla saw no one except Georgia. 'You had to do it. Had to ruin everything. If anyone could do it, it would be you! I knew you shouldn't have been my matron of honour but my father had to have his way. Well I'm not the only one who's a laughing stock. Serves him right.'

'I'm so sorry, Tayla.' Georgia wilted against the pillows and closed her eyes, and Max realised that the ridiculous behaviour of Tayla was upsetting the new mother.

'You will be!' Tayla spat, and Max stepped away from the wall.

'That's enough.' His voice was very quiet but sliced off Tayla's words as if he'd swathed his arm through the air like a conductor. Tayla froze before turning slowly to face him.

'Max?' She stamped her foot and another tiny white feather puffed into the air. 'I knew you must have stayed with her.'

'Obviously,' he drawled, and then regretted his provocativeness for Georgia's sake. Outside work interference it was probably the first time he'd made the effort to check Tayla. Maybe he had let everything slide too much in his obsession to land this job.

'Look at your suit!' Tayla was slow to see the dangerous glint in Max's eye. 'And why did you have to be the one to go with her? There were half a dozen obstetricians there but, no, you had to leave me at the altar like a fool.'

Max glanced across at Georgia and the sleeping baby. 'I'm sorry about your wedding, Tayla,' he said. 'But perhaps in private and later.'

Tayla faltered and stretched her face into a smile, finally connecting Max's displeasure. 'It was your wedding, too.' The plaintive note sounded clearly. 'And the magazine was there taking photos. No wonder we couldn't find you when the ambulance turned up. When it was called off my father searched everywhere for you.'

'Your father would have done better to spend his time checking on his new great-niece.' Max raised his eyebrows. 'I'm sure you, too, were concerned that Georgia's baby almost lost her life.'

Tayla glanced at the baby in Georgia's arms with barely concealed disinterest. 'Of course.' She dragged her arm across her face. 'It's been such a horrible morning. I think they will still print the photos from the church but as a disaster now. I've been quite distraught.' And quietly she began to sob.

Max dropped his jaw in amazement and Georgia shifted her baby up to her shoulder and slid to the edge of the bed.

In sudden clarity Max realised if he didn't step in Georgia would rise from her bed to comfort her cousin and take all the blame for something that no one could have prevented.

'Stay there, Georgia. Rest. You've had a big morning, too. I'll take Tayla away and calm her down.'

Tayla lifted her head and he admitted she cried very prettily but some of the sterling reasons he'd had for marrying her had strangely seeped away.

'Come on, Tayla,' he said more gently. She really had been excited about the magazine shoot and he needed to be more patient. 'I'll make you a coffee in the consultants' tearoom and we can talk.' He turned her towards the door and glanced over his shoulder at the woman in the bed.

'Look after Thor.'

The sweetness of his smile made the lump of tears in Georgia's chest swell even more and she nodded stupidly and watched him leave.

She'd have to name her daughter or she'd begun to think of her as Thor. The problem was she'd only chosen boys names. More reason to dislike the inaccuracy of ultrasounds.

Actually, she would like to call her Maxine but no doubt the affinity she felt towards a certain obstetrician would pass. She was never falling for that again.

She wouldn't be calling her daughter after her father because the memories of Sol's dangerous possessiveness left her quivering in her bed. She shuddered and forced her mind back to the present.

Her daughter was like a little lioness with her roar and her power and her aggressive hold on life. No man would try to run her life. She should call her Elsa after the lioness in *Born Free*. Actually, she liked that. She liked it a lot.

'Hello, Elsa.' Elsa opened one dark blue eye and glared at her mother before thick black lashes fluttered down again and she drifted back to sleep.

Well, that was settled. She looked up as a knock sounded at the door and her uncle poked his head around it.

'You available for visitors?'

'Come in, Harry.' She gestured to the seat beside the bed and her nearest living relative sank onto the hard plastic with relief. He peered at the baby in her arms.

'So she's well? No ill effects from her dramatic entry into the world?' He lifted one finger and stroked the baby's soft hair.

'The paediatrician said she'll be fine. Because Elsa was so vigorous at birth, we're sure she coped with whatever fall in oxygen she suffered.'

Harry raised his bushy white eyebrows. 'Elsa. Strong name. Still, you must have been terrified. I'm glad you're both well. I gather Max did a great job.'

'He was very calm and caught her beautifully.' She leaned towards her uncle. 'I'm so sorry about Tayla's wedding.'

'Water under the bridge.' He looked at her and they both smiled at the poor pun. 'Tayla threw hysterics in the church when the limo drove off. I was glad to get out of there.'

Georgia bit her lip. She felt too guilty to smile at her uncle's dry amusement. 'She's with Max now. I'm sure he'll calm her down.'

'She'd better show a more attractive side than I saw this morning or it won't matter how much he needs a wife.' Her uncle looked at Georgia quickly and then away.

'I did not say that.' Distressed, he rubbed his gnarled hands together. He was a self-made success and proud of his hands, but he wasn't proud of that slip. 'I'm an old man and get mixed up sometimes.'

He looked around the room—anywhere but at Georgia. 'You look after young Elsa here and I'll see you soon.' Harry bent down and kissed her cheek before he lumbered out of the room as fast as he could.

Georgia stared after him. 'Good grief,' she said out loud. 'What do you make of that, Elsa?'

'So you've named her?' Max spoke from the door. Georgia looked serene and competent with the baby nestled in her arms, and he stifled the pang of pain he'd thought he'd got over about not having children.

Imagine someone like her to come home to after work. During his engagement Max had eventually realised that at best Tayla would fly to visit him every few weeks and he'd accepted she would continue with her life as charity social queen.

At the time it had seemed enough because he could never offer a maternal woman a family and Tayla made no secret of the fact that she didn't want children. A realistic Tayla was better than the beauties who had chorused that IVF would do the trick.

Imagine if it had been possible to marry someone like Georgia? They could have even worked together and he'd have a real insight into the care the women were receiving.

Enough. He wouldn't be searching for another wife. One close shave was enough. Maybe he could run his disastrous day past the board and they'd consider his circumstances against the fact he wasn't married. He'd sort something out.

He frowned at the strange expression on

Georgia's face and he wondered what new complication had arisen.

For Georgia, after the first quick glance, she didn't know where to look. Perhaps she'd caught her uncle's affliction of avoiding eye contact, but this was a bit awkward after hearing Max needed a wife.

She flicked another peek at him and away again. 'Harry just left.'

'Yes, I know.' Max frowned. 'I saw him but he seemed in a bit of a hurry. I'm not sure he's speaking to me after I failed so dismally as a son-in-law.'

Georgia winced and looked down as Elsa slept contentedly in her arms. That was definitely her fault. She wished her daughter would wake up and yell. At least she could avoid conversation then. Her brain was spinning from Harry's bombshell. Max just didn't seem the type to need a wife.

The guy had everything. Looks, money, fabulous career. A sliver of ice slid down her back. Maybe he wanted to own a trophy wife, like Sol had.

'How is Tayla?' It was all she could think of to say.

'Unengaged. She doesn't want to marry me any more.' Max dropped the words into the room like an afterthought. 'But she'll be fine. I've sent her home with my brother. I think they will do very well together. We don't normally get on but Paul's been a godsend this week.'

Georgia frowned and played back his comment

in her mind. Unengaged. Needed a wife. 'Did you say the wedding is off?'

'Definitely. I couldn't guarantee to her I would never rush off like that again and she said it wasn't good enough.'

'She's a fool.' Georgia had thought the words and somehow they slipped quietly into the room for Max to hear.

'I think so—but there you have it.' He was irrepressible and she couldn't help smiling. They both grinned at each other and the camaraderie was back.

Georgia decided she must have misunderstood Uncle Harry. Max didn't seem too upset for someone who needed to have a wife. She would go with her instincts and her instincts said Max Beresford could be trusted.

'So why were you marrying Tayla if you didn't love her?'

He sighed and sat down. She realised he was dressed in theatre garb so he must have changed out of his soiled suit at some time. He pulled his hand over his strong chin as she watched him gather his thoughts.

'The board of directors for the new job were adamant. They wanted me but no wife, no job. Tayla seemed like a good idea at the time.'

Georgia felt disappointment lodge in her throat. She was a damn poor judge of character. The man was shallow. 'Not a good reason to tie yourself to one person for the rest of your life.'

'It was only for a year if it didn't work out.' He

looked up at her and smiled sympathetically. 'I gather your foray into married life wasn't a roaring success either.'

She wasn't the one who needed the sympathy. 'I believed in commitment when I took my vows.'

'And how was your marriage?' The gentle tone in which he asked the question made her eyes sting with sudden tears.

She did not want to go there. 'None of your business.'

'That bad, eh?' He pressed his lips together as if holding back further comment, and suddenly she could at least admit how bad it had been to herself.

It was her turn to sigh. 'Worse. How did you know?'

He shrugged his shoulders slightly. 'From something you said when you were in labour about not missing Elsa's father.'

The limo ride came back to her in Technicolor and she shuddered. 'Labour. Could you call that labour? That horrific few minutes when I thought I would lose my baby?'

She shook her head. 'That was like being hit by a truck.' She couldn't begin to imagine the desolation she would be going through now if Elsa hadn't survived. 'I haven't thanked you for being there when I needed someone.'

Max smiled. 'And I haven't thanked you for saving me from Tayla. So now we have that out of the way, let's forget the others. What are you going to do now?'

Georgia tilted her head. 'My situation is fine. I'm free. I have a healthy baby, a home and a nanny arranged for the future when I go back to work.'

He looked a little taken aback at her well-laid plans. What had he expected?

'I can see you are organised.' He stood up. 'And you must be tired. I'll go. Congratulations on your beautiful daughter. My best wishes to both of you. Good bye.' He smiled and left.

She watched him go, watched him walk out after all they had been through, and now she really was alone. Well, what had she expected? He wasn't even her cousin-in-law now so she probably wouldn't ever see him again.

Of course, she couldn't sleep after that.

Elsa woke and gratefully Georgia fed her and stroked her hair and began to feel the peace she'd dreamt of when her child was safely born.

She tried to imagine how she would have felt if Max hadn't been there and she'd been alone when Elsa had been born. If Elsa hadn't been fine. It didn't bear thinking about.

Then the cold ice of fear in the base of her stomach reminded her there were other things to be afraid of. What if Sol came back and tried to take Elsa, as he'd threatened? Could she keep her baby safe? Could Max help her keep her baby safe? It was a dangerous thought.

The next morning Dr Sol Winton stepped out of the lifts on the maternity floor and no one tried to stop him. The quality of his suit and the half-exposed stethoscope poking out of his pocket ensured that nobody questioned he belonged there.

He inclined his head at two nurses and his slow smile brought the colour to both their cheeks. The gilt-ribboned chocolate boxes screamed money and he placed one box on the nurse's desk and kept one in his hand.

'I'm looking for my wife. Georgia Winton?'

'Certainly, Doctor. She's in room four, down the corridor on the left.'

'Thank you. Enjoy the chocolates.'

He set off as if sure of his welcome. A tall, well-dressed, charming man, who drew the eyes of women and exuded authority.

When he entered the room only the baby was there wrapped up in a bunny rug in the Perspex cot. A name card tucked into the end read, 'Elsa, baby of Georgia, five pounds two ounces.'

He reached across and stroked the baby's cheek and her downy skin was silky soft beneath his finger.

CHAPTER THREE

MAX FROWNED and strode quickly down the corridor as he saw the man enter Georgia's room.

He knew most of the consultants across the hospital but not this one. Some latent protective instinct raised the hairs on the back of his neck and all he could think about was that Georgia might need him.

His suspicions firmed at the sight of the man bent over Elsa's cot.

Max loomed in the doorway. His voice came out low and hard. 'Can I help you?'

Sol straightened slowly and he lifted his chin. 'No. I don't think so. Thank you.'

The man smiled but something about his phoney amusement increased Max's own wariness and disquiet.

Max moved to one side of the doorway to allow a free exit from the room—though only if the man left Elsa in her cot.

'Are you a friend of Georgia's?' Max enquired

politely, yet the hint of steel suggested it wasn't a frivolous question and he required an answer.

'I'm more than that.' Sol smiled gently. 'Are you her doctor?'

'You could say that.' Max looked up as Georgia opened the bathroom door and his instincts firmed as her eyes widened and then closed for a second as if her worst nightmare had come true.

Her hand hovered over her mouth. 'Sol?' She shook her head but no further words came.

'My dear wife.' Sol smiled.

Georgia shook her head again and the words burst out in a vehement whisper. 'I'm not your wife.'

Sol smiled again, and from the outside he looked quite pleasant yet something made Max take a step closer to Georgia in support.

Sol ignored him. 'You'll always be my wife. But I do see this is not a good time so I'll leave you. Our daughter is beautiful.' He placed the chocolates squarely on the bedside table.

'Good day.' He turned nonchalantly and sauntered away.

Georgia belted the robe as she rushed to Elsa to check she was fine. 'Thank God you were here.'

Fighting back tears, she looked at Max. 'Did he try to take her?' She lifted and hugged Elsa to her as she sank onto the bed as if unable to support the weight on her legs. Her hands shook violently.

Max didn't know what to do to comfort her.

'No. He didn't pick Elsa up. He just looked at

her.' What the hell was all that about? Max thought, and he glanced at the door through which Sol had disappeared. He'd love to ask the sleaze but he'd gone and Georgia needed him.

Max sat down beside Georgia on the bed and slid his arm around her shoulders. She quivered under his arm like a new lamb.

'I'll put safeguards in place. Your ex-husband won't be able to get to you if that's what you want.'

She shook her head and shuddered as she wrapped her arms around her baby. 'I don't want to stay here.'

Max squeezed her shoulders. 'Where do you want to go?' Her distress affected him in a way he hadn't expected and he'd like to have shaken the truth out of the other man.

Georgia's free hand was at her throat. She could barely speak because of the panic she was trying to control. 'I was afraid this would happen. There is something I need to explain. Something I haven't told anybody.'

She hesitated with reluctance to dwell on the whole distressing nightmare but it had to be spoken of. Her reluctance had almost cost the ultimate price. Elsa.

Sol would take her baby if he possibly could. He'd threatened her in those silky tones of his and the thought terrified her, made her sick to her stomach, and now it grew to epic proportions, like a phobia about spiders—except her phobia was all about Sol.

Even what he had done to her before was nothing to this fear that he might take her baby, and even though a tiny spark deep in her brain whispered she was being irrational, she had no control over the dread that was rising in her throat.

Georgia drew a deep breath and her voice sounded weak and strained even to her own ears.

No wonder Sol could smile.

And no doubt Max would hear the paranoia too but there was nothing she could do about that except try and master it at a later time when she had time to regroup. At this moment she just needed Max to understand.

She hadn't progressed to why that seemed so important at this moment.

'Before I met Sol I was happy in my work, a senior midwife in my unit and studying for my master's in midwifery.'

Max nodded. 'Harry said you were well respected and then you became sick—is that right?'

'In the end I began to think I was sick. I need to start the story before then.'

She closed her eyes for a second to gather her thoughts. 'I met my husband, the new senior consultant at our hospital, Sol Winton, and he swept me off my feet. He promised nothing would change, and marriage would only enhance my full life, and that he couldn't live without me.'

She laughed without amusement. 'I was flattered. I'd passed thirty waiting for Mr Right. I'm no raving beauty and he was distinguished, handsome, and I'd begun to think I'd missed out on love and marriage and children. He caught me at a vulnerable time and I thought I loved him.

'In truth I was married for two years to a man who wanted to own me, body and soul, and rule my life down to the smallest degree.

'In the beginning I believed his excessive protectiveness was because he treasured me but I soon realised it was because he felt I was his prized possession and he was training me to jump.'

Georgia drew a shuddering breath and her shoulders shook until Max edged back closer and leant against her. 'You OK?'

The tremor stopped and she nodded. 'I don't like to go over it but I have to so that you'll understand.'

Max shook his head. 'Not if you don't want to.'

'I have to,' she said with resolve.

'OK.' Max pressed harder against her as if he knew she needed that support.

She felt strangely safer with Max's hip and shoulders touching hers, which was ridiculous but it helped her to go on. 'I tried to make Sol see that marriage wasn't a power game and I needed to be my own person, but my charming ex-husband, the highly esteemed obstetrician, informed everyone I was a paranoid depressive. That's not an easy thing to dispute if you have reason to be unhappy.'

'That would explain what Harry said about your marriage getting you down.'

'Harry mentioned it, did he?'

She saw the look on Max's face and sighed. 'This

is what I meant about disputing people's opinions. Sol made it seem I protested too much.'

Max frowned. 'It's OK. I believe you. Go on.'

'I was a professional woman with a career and friends before Sol. But he became more and more demanding. He isolated me from my friends and began to dictate my daily routine. He would change it at a whim.' She clutched Elsa to her as she remembered.

'He cancelled my appointments with my uni, pulled my shifts so that when I turned up, cases had been replaced by another midwife, and that was when I realised people had begun to talk. He'd arranged a visit to a psychiatrist and circulated that I suffered from an anxiety-driven mental illness. The saddest thing was that I almost began to believe him, but I kept telling myself it was his problem, not mine, and refused to take medication. Finally I left him.'

'Leaving was a good thing.' Max nodded.

'I left him for a year but I had to stay at the hospital because they were paying for my master's. The day the divorce papers hit Sol's desk he upped his campaign to win me back but I knew I would never go back to him. That was when he finally realised it wasn't just another extended game.'

She laughed without humour. 'Sol wanted me back, and had everyone at work on his side, and then he threatened my best friend's credibility over a drug order that he'd tampered with. He'd moved on to blackmail.'

'So prove it.'

'It was her word and mine against Sol's, and he said he'd drop his case if I went back to him.'

'You went back?' Max leaned forward incredulously.

'I thought I had it all worked out. I prepared safeguards against any problems. I was going to stay with him until she was safe. Stay only until she couldn't be charged.'

She looked away so he couldn't read her face.

She didn't mention the horror of what Sol had forced her to endure and that she doubted she'd ever want to make love with a man again.

She didn't mention the fact that she woke up at night in a lather of sweat and a pounding heart. Or that now she had an even bigger fear. 'Well, in the end, she wasn't charged. I left again. Later I found out I was pregnant.'

Max raised his eyebrows. 'Why didn't you discredit him?'

'Sol is a powerful man. People believe him.' Georgia could feel palpitations in her chest and unconsciously she rested her hand there. He'd said he would take her baby at birth. He'd said he would if she didn't come back.

All the old fears and uncertainties and even unreasonable guilt that she'd heaped on herself began to surface and she fought to keep them away. She needed to conquer this. Elsa needed her to conquer this. 'It seemed easier just to leave and never go back.'

Max muttered an oath under his breath.

She went on because the sooner she did so, the sooner she could stop thinking about those horrible few weeks.

'Sol had been here to tell Harry I was depressed and paranoid. He covered himself in case I told them what he was really like. He is very plausible and dangerous.

'When Harry suggested I move in with them, I decided it would be good for my baby to know family because she would never know her father if I could help it.' She kissed the top of her daughter's head.

She could see Max was trying to understand and at least he was trying. It was more than a lot of other people did.

Max squeezed her shoulder. 'We'll all help you feel safe again.'

She looked at him and he read the disbelief in her face. 'A month ago I received a repeated threat on my mobile phone against my unborn child. He would find a way to take her if I didn't come back to him,' she whispered.

That wiped the smile off Max's face and he felt his hand tighten protectively over her shoulder. 'Mongrel.'

She sighed under his arm. 'The police said nothing could be proved because Sol had used a public phone to make the call. All I could do was change my number.'

Max shook his head. 'He's put you through hell. I wish I'd known when I had him here.'

She shuddered. 'He's seen her now. I'm losing control of my life again. I left Sol because I needed to get control back.' She looked at him with determination in her eyes. 'And I will. I am. Just.

'I decided to move here and start again because I need family for my baby and I can make a good life for myself and my daughter. But now I'm scared again.'

He could help her. He felt the shift. She needed help and his gut tightened. He barely knew the woman but suddenly it all felt ordained. No doubt there would be flak along the way and the ex-husband sounded like a loony, but suddenly all that was unimportant if he could protect her. There was something about Georgia that he truly admired and was irresistibly drawn to.

Now their closeness during Elsa's dramatic birth and today's near abduction made him realise that she probably needed him more than he needed her.

Win-win situation.

It was a strangely satisfying feeling for Max that had nothing to do with suddenly being eligible for the job again if she agreed. That he could protect Georgia was paramount. 'We could help each other.'

Georgia looked up at him. 'How?'

'Your divorce was finalized, wasn't it?' He tilted his head hopefully.

'Yes. I made sure that happened.' She frowned.

'Why?' The guy bounced all over the place and she couldn't keep up. 'I'm beginning to think Tayla had a lucky escape.'

He shrugged. 'Tayla was getting exactly what she wanted. An indulgent life with me to parade every now and then at her charity functions, and I had a wife I needed for my job. Neither of us planned on having children.'

No children, no living together, all for the sake of a job. What was wrong with these people? 'Wrong era,' she said, with barely concealed distaste. 'Employers can't make you marry any more.'

Max shrugged. 'The directors wanted a married man because they've had so many problems with people leaving the role. The last one ran off and eloped when he was most needed. The powers that choose knew of my impending marriage and that gave me the edge.'

He shrugged. 'Unfortunately, the idea of living with Tayla just won't gel any more for me either.' He said the words as if he he'd decided to change his brand of deodorant.

'And you're telling me this because…?' She couldn't keep the disappointment out of her voice. She'd liked him and he wasn't worthy of that. Despite everything, she still believed true love was out there for most people, and Max cheapened it when he talked like that.

He lifted his head and captured her gaze with his own as if he sensed her disapproval and it mattered to him. His golden eyes warmed. 'I'd been having second thoughts about marrying Tayla earlier. Even before your water broke.'

Georgia winced at the memory of that time in the church. That certainly wouldn't go down as a highlight of her life!

He grinned. 'Don't be squeamish. You're a midwife. As an obstetrician I think labour is great, as long as your baby is due.'

She watched him pull himself back to the topic, and she had to smile as he went on.

'You've made me realise how close I'd been to disaster with Tayla. I can see now I want more in a wife than convenient paperwork.'

How had they started this conversation? Now she was confused at a time when she most needed clarity. 'You want to tell me what you want in a wife?' Suddenly she felt like crying. She knew what she didn't need in a husband.

He went on and she tried to blink away her tears before he could see them.

Max was getting to the point. He just hoped she saw it the way he did. 'Ah. Yes. The big question. Now I want a partner. Someone who understands what I do and even has a passion for it. I can't fight Tayla every time someone has a baby out of hours or obstetrics have an emergency.'

He noticed the way her hand tightened over her baby and he couldn't begin to imagine how she must feel to have been so close to losing her daughter a second time.

Maybe he had stumbled on someone he could come home to or meet at work and bounce problems off. Someone who had a social conscience and a warm heart. Someone like Georgia.

He couldn't help the glimmer of hope that maybe the last twenty-four hours had all worked out the way they had for a reason—or with divine intervention, as requested.

No doubt he was mad, but the idea he'd just had wouldn't leave. He could even salvage the job from something Georgia had said if he played up the business aspect, but suddenly that wasn't as important as protecting Georgia from the creep. He paused and looked at her again. 'You could marry me.'

She held up her hand. 'You don't know me.'

He sat forward. 'I know enough. I'm sure you are a sensible woman and wouldn't normally entertain the idea. That's why I'm pursuing you now when your guard is down.'

She huffed humourlessly. 'My guard isn't down that much. I've just seen my ex-husband and my protective instinct hormones are surging. I don't need to waste another couple of years of my life finding out if the next guy I marry is a jerk, or worse.'

She had a point, but Max didn't believe he was a jerk. 'What about a temporary marriage with, say, a year's contract? You save me and I'll protect you.' He frowned with concentration as he marshalled his best arguments.

'I'm serious, Georgia. I need to be married and after today I only have one week left. I've a friend I can get a dispensation form to get a licence in forty-eight hours, and you would be out of your ex's reach until you are stronger.'

He sat back a little in case he was crowding her. 'It doesn't look like I will fall madly in love at my age and I like you. I like you a lot. I need a temporary wife and Harry said you were looking for a job after the baby. You could work with me when you're ready.'

'It all sounds so coldly clinical.'

'We could warm it up.' He saw her face close and he backed off quickly. 'I'm sorry. Joking. We won't go there.' He paused and risked a lighter comment. 'Especially as you've just given birth.'

She had to smile and he knew it. But he was intrigued.

'Would it help if I told you I think we would deal very well together? Much better than expected?'

'Much better than whom?' She shook her head. 'You and Tayla? Two selfish, immature, rich people who think marriage is a sham or an excuse to wear feathers?'

He held up his hands. 'The feathers were not my idea. In fact, a condition of marrying me is that you are not allowed to wear feathers.'

'I'm not marrying you, Max.' She turned her shoulder on him. 'I'm not even sure I like you after this conversation. And I can't believe that Harry was a part of this whole sell-my-daughter-to-a-loveless-marriage thing.'

'Harry wanted to have Tayla safely married before he was much older.'

He saw the moment she understood, and the sudden sadness in her eyes as she sat back against him, all else forgotten. 'Why the urgency?'

'That's for Harry to tell, not me.' It was Harry's secret, not his.

'Poor Uncle Harry.'

He squeezed her shoulder. 'Leave it. He is dealing with this in his own way.'

She stared and shook her head. 'So that's why Harry agreed?'

'One of the reasons.' He smiled sympathetically and then went off at a tangent again. 'I do have one burning question that's puzzled me.'

She raised her eyebrows and his arm slid away from her shoulder so he could look at her fully.

'Did you want a place in the wedding party or did Harry lean on you?'

She grimaced. 'Who wants to be a pregnant matron of honour? Harry was so pleased that Tayla was settling down, and he wanted to see that, as cousins, his daughter and I were friends. Knowing he's unwell explains why he was so insistent. I wanted to please Harry and the idea that I did have a family was comforting.'

Max admired her warmth for Harry. 'Harry thought I would make a good husband.'

'I understand that.' She looked worriedly at him.

'I've already made one mistake in marriage, though, and I'm frightened I'd make a bigger one with you.'

Max could feel the swing his way and he vowed she wouldn't regret it. 'That's the beauty of it, Georgia. This is a business arrangement.'

Her voice was quiet but determined. She spoke slowly. 'I'm thinking. I can't believe I'm doing it but I am considering your proposal on the basis of a one-year contract.'

She shivered under his arm. 'My biggest problem is that I'm still frightened. Especially now Elsa has been born. Sol has seen her, and will want her. And me. I'm too vulnerable.'

She looked up at him to read his face and make sure he understood what she was offering. To make clear all she wasn't offering and the risks.

She spelt it out. 'In a business relationship I could build up my strength in a safe environment and you need a wife in name only. To be honest, that's all I've got to offer anyway. And I need to ease back to work and get on with my life.'

He squeezed her shoulders and she felt so frail under his hand. He would guard them both. 'Fine. Come home with me and I swear I will keep you both safe.'

He smiled crookedly because he didn't want to say it but in all honesty it needed to be said. 'I don't wish to take advantage of your shock unfairly. Your uncle would probably also be able to offer you protection from your ex-husband.'

She shook her head. 'That won't work. You say

Harry is unwell and I'm not up to Tayla's recriminations.'

'Not a relaxing thought.' He smiled at her and the tension lightened a little in the room. That was it, then. He had what he wanted. Hopefully so did she. He stood up. 'Let's go, then.'

She tilted her head and looked up at him. 'It's that easy?'

'It will be. You pack and I'll sort out the rest.'

She shifted Elsa onto one arm and pulled the toothbrush from her pocket. 'I'm packed.'

When Georgia walked out of the hospital and into the sunlight it felt as if Tayla's disastrous wedding had been a year ago not just one day.

Max's hand hovered near the small of her back and she carried Elsa tightly against her, as if to defend her from an unknown assailant.

Incredibly, with Max, she did feel safe, even after the shock of knowing Sol had found her.

'Why do I feel so protected with you when I barely know you?' She'd met him such a short time ago and she'd made a disastrous marriage before. Was she making another mistake?

'Because I'm a mature and respected consultant,' he said. 'I've known Harry for years and your uncle trusted me enough to marry his only daughter off to me.'

That part sounded acceptable.

Then she saw Max's big square, ostentatious, boy's toy shiny black Hummer parked outside the door and she shook her head. 'You're just a kid with your ego.'

Max patted the bonnet of the huge all-terrain vehicle. 'Cool, isn't it? At least I get my baby dirty when I go offroad.'

'Where's your chauffeur?'

'He has other jobs. I don't use that car often. It belongs to my mother.'

She sniffed and looked again at the vehicle. 'Does your baby have an infant capsule?'

He smirked. 'Now she does.'

She looked at him. 'When did you get the time to organise that?'

'The capsule belongs to Maternity and I promised I'd have it back tomorrow.'

'You have connections.'

'I'm one big connection, but to answer your question...' He paused and looked her full in the face. 'You trust me with Elsa, don't you?'

'Of course.'

'Then you can trust me with you as well.'

She had no answer for that.

CHAPTER FOUR

MAX and Georgia's wedding was simple, at the registry office, and the only guests were Max's housekeeper and Harry.

It was done two days later, as soon as the licence came through, and Georgia didn't wear feathers.

As she stood beside her new husband and watched him sign the marriage certificate, she realised how little she knew about this man. And yet even in the last forty-eight hours he had shown a kindness and sensitivity that brought tears to her eyes. Hormones again, of course, but nonetheless Max was a darling and even Elsa liked him.

Goodness knew what he had told Harry, but her uncle had nothing good to say about Sol and kept patting her on the shoulder. What could have been horribly awkward as they arranged their hurried wedding and transfer north proved an amusing and relaxed time, thanks to Max.

They moved north to Coffs Harbour straight after the ceremony.

* * *

Living with Max was an experience. Where Sol had been obsessive about cleanliness and order, Max was oblivious and gloriously extravagant.

He thought nothing of dropping towels by the pool, having his St Bernard in the house, and arriving with an enormous bunch of bananas to hang on the veranda.

Thankfully he had an eccentric housekeeper, Mrs White, who adored him and didn't mind.

For the first six weeks of Elsa's life, Max ensured that Georgia had little to do except be there for her baby, eat well-cooked meals provided by the amazing Mrs White, and sleep in between attending to Elsa's needs.

Thank goodness, because Elsa roared and screamed and barely slept with colic for most of that time, and Georgia shuddered when she thought of how it would have been if she'd had to manage a household as well.

The first night Elsa had screamed, Max had just come in from an emergency Caesarean at two a.m. and Georgia had been down in the kitchen to try Elsa with some boiled water in a bottle.

Max had found Georgia nightie-clad and barefoot, her thick hair pushed distractedly behind her ears, and every time Elsa had emitted a tiny broken sob he'd seen it had torn at her mother's heart.

'Give her to me.' He held out his hands and he saw the way she hesitated. It was amazing how much that hurt. 'I do know about babies, you know.'

'Of course you do.' She passed Elsa over and he hated her hesitation to trust him.

Distraught and exhausted, Georgia looked at her wits' end and Max just wanted to hug her.

Georgia ran her fingers through her hair. 'But so do I! I know more about babies than you,' she said, and there was a break in her voice. 'But it's not working!'

Baby Elsa felt tense and coiled with pain in his arms, and he saw why being unable to comfort her daughter would upset Georgia so badly.

She watched him like a hawk as he cupped her baby's head in his hands and rested her body on his forearms. Then he propped her bottom against his stomach so that she was folded with her legs up his chest. He'd seen the midwives carry babies this way at night when they had pain. When Elsa stopped crying, Georgia rolled her eyes.

'Typical,' she said, and he couldn't help the smirk.

'See.'

'Hmmm.' She crossed to the sink and filled a glass with water. 'You can hold her while I have two headache tablets for the damage caused by the last two hours.'

'Have a hot chocolate. I'll join you. Little missy here looks like she wants to sleep.'

Georgia sniffed. 'She inherited it from her mother, who also wants to sleep.' Georgia literally drooped in front of him and his need to comfort her returned. Normally she was so efficient, he actually admired her more for being human.

'Forget the chocolate. Why don't you grab a couple of hours' rest? I imagine you've not long fed her so she'll probably sleep until morning if the pain leaves her alone. I can bring her back to you when she wakes up.'

'You've been up all night and you have to work tomorrow.' He saw the struggle with the concept of leaving her baby with him.

'Tomorrow is Saturday and I'm only on call.' He watched her rub her forehead as she tried to concentrate.

'Saturday. So it is.' She smiled wearily and he felt his gut contract at her vulnerability.

The more he saw of her the more he just wanted to pull her into his arms and protect her from her own stubborn, independent self. And a few other things crossed his mind like freight trains, but he wasn't going there.

The last things she needed from him were pressure and lust, and he'd promised himself he would leave her to heal the deep wounds left by her former husband for at least the year.

He didn't know if he'd last that long but he was going to damn well try, if it killed him.

By the time Elsa was smiling and cooing at two months Georgia felt as if she'd lived in Max's wonderful house for ever—but it wasn't the real world.

She saw very little of Max, though, except when

he appeared in the early hours to give her a break if Elsa was having a bad night. Even at those times she was usually so exhausted she just handed Elsa over and crashed into her bed so she felt that she knew less about him than she had when they'd first met.

He was unfailingly polite, wonderful with Elsa considering he had no real experience of babies apart from helping them into the world, and provided the safest haven a woman in need could wish for.

The disconcerting thing about Max for Georgia was the speed with which he seemed to disappear. She knew he was busy at work but she wondered if that, in fact, accounted for his hurry to get away. She really would have liked to have seen more of him.

In the tenth week Georgia had had enough of being the lady of leisure and Max's avoidance techniques had begun to irk her.

On the day it all changed, she wandered into the kitchen in search of Mrs White while Max was away at work. She found another potato peeler to help with the vegetables and prepared her assault. 'What time will Max be home tonight, Mrs White?'

Mrs White, who would not be diverted from calling Georgia Mrs Beresford, or allow Georgia to call her Miriam, was a little round woman who, despite her name, dyed her short hair jet-black and wore heavy eyeliner.

She looked up from her own peeler and smiled at Georgia like a jolly panda. 'It's Monday so they have a regional discussion at five. Probably seven-thirty or maybe eight tonight.'

'He works long hours, doesn't he?'

'Always has, but he used to try to get away off-roading on weekends.' She pointed her peeler at Georgia. 'Though he hasn't had the Hummer out in the bush since we moved up here.'

Georgia knew Mrs White didn't understand their relationship. Obviously the housekeeper was aware they slept in separate rooms and usually ate meals at different times because of Elsa's regime. They weren't even housemates as such because their paths rarely crossed.

But Mrs White had seen they were happy enough and that was good as far as she was concerned, especially compared to the close shave of Tayla—an opinion she'd shared with Georgia very early on.

For Georgia, the initial space Max had given her had been perfect, but now the distance he'd created frustrated the life out of her.

It was like living in the snow with a big, roaring fire on the other side of the window she wasn't even allowed to warm her hands at. His company was becoming more desirable all the time.

If she didn't want to fall into the trap of building her life around the flashes of company Max gave her then it was time to begin to think of a few hours of work or she would never regain her independence.

'I'd like to share my evening meal with Max from now on, if that's OK. Elsa is starting to go to sleep by seven. Perhaps I could set the table in the dining room tonight.'

Mrs White didn't quite clap her hands but she did beam approvingly. 'Of course. I'm sure he'd enjoy the company.' She smiled across at her. 'And if Elsa wakes up, I could mind her so you won't be interrupted during your dinner.'

Georgia opened her mouth to demur when she realised that if she was interrupted then Max would be also, and she could see Mrs White was keen on the idea.

'Thank you. That would be lovely.'

When Max arrived home that evening, the table was set for two. Georgia had taken the trouble to dress for dinner and put make-up on for the first time in over two months.

She felt like a schoolgirl on her first date, which was ridiculous when she considered how up close and personal she and Max had been at Elsa's birth.

When he first came in, Georgia felt a fluttery tingle of excitement reverberate through her, just by looking at the way he smiled at seeing her. He looked tall and handsome and his white shirt sat snugly across his shoulders and chest in a disconcertingly sexy way.

His smile held a hint of surprise when he saw the table, but the expression was there so fleetingly she couldn't be sure, and she hoped it was a pleasant change for him and not one of those save-me-from-the-nuisance moments.

'I thought I might join you for dinner in the evenings if work permits, Max. Is that all right with you?' Georgia heard the uncertainty in her voice and she winced. It wasn't like she was asking to sleep with the guy.

'I'd like that. We don't seem to have seen much of each other.' His eyes crinkled and his golden eyes warmed as his gaze drifted over her. 'You look beautiful.'

'Thank you.' She didn't know what else to say but some of the nervousness in her stomach subsided.

The conversation faltered and they both looked out the window.

Max broke into the silence. 'Elsa seems to be settling with her colic.'

Georgia winced. She'd felt so guilty about that. 'It must have been very distracting for you, and I am sorry.'

Max smiled that particularly sweet smile that always brought a lump to Georgia's throat. 'It has been very distracting to have a gorgeous ghost wandering around my house in the early hours of the morning. I'd grown used to her, though, and actually quite miss bumping into her in the wee small hours.'

Georgia began to relax. 'I'd think myself more of a gargoyle than gorgeous, but I did feel like a ghost in those early days. You were pretty wonderful with Elsa.'

'Nonsense,' Max said. 'She liked me.'

Georgia pretended to glare at him. 'Excuse me.

She liked me, too, but she would not stop crying sometimes.'

He tilted his head. 'Ah, no. There is a difference. She adores you and knows you feel her pain.' He smiled again. 'I'm just the shallow bloke she can go to sleep with when she's too tired to cry. But I think she's grown out of me now.'

Georgia couldn't imagine anyone growing out of Max. He was such a sweetie.

She'd been going to edge slowly towards discussing her plans but it seemed too complicated. Suddenly she just needed to get it all out into the open.

'I want to go back to work, Max. One or two days a week. Or even half-days, if I could. That way, I can come home to Elsa for feeds.'

Max nodded but he felt like shaking his head. Violently. He looked at her and thought Georgia had grown even more stunning over the last two months. He was having a hard time keeping her out of his thoughts at work, and the idea of her on the hospital ward would complicate things enormously.

'Are you sure it's not too soon?' he said quietly, and he passed her the lemon squash with ice she always seemed to ask for on the rare occasions they shared a drink in the evenings.

It was hot up here, he'd noticed that, and now they wanted him to do three months past Murwillumbah near the Queensland border. They'd actually asked if his wife would be interested in a little part-time work. That would be an even smaller hospital to run into her in.

'I'm bored, Max. I'm sick of living off you. I want to regain my independence. Elsa doesn't need me twenty-four hours a day now. Mrs White would love to have her to herself for a couple of hours in the daytime.'

Georgia paused and then said, 'Thanks to you, I feel safe, Max. And ready to do more.'

Max nodded. 'You're the one who has to decide. If you think you're ready then I'm sure you are. I'll ask around tomorrow.'

He poured himself a glass of beer. 'I've had an offer for three months up past Murwillumbah where the one obstetric GP has retired. The idea would be to take over his practice for a few weeks but really they'd want me to see if it is still viable as a maternity unit. It's pretty much a midwifery-run unit and almost in Queensland. If I go, would you want to come or stay here with Mrs White?'

'Is she staying here?' Georgia looked startled and he wondered why.

'She will do if you do!' Georgia had more need of Mrs White with Elsa than he did.

'I'm a big girl. You have to stop looking after me, Max.'

'You're my wife,' he said. In truth, he did very little and would love to do more, but she valued her independence and the other thing, the one he tried not to think about but kept him awake at night, needed time.

'In name only,' she said.

Bingo. That was the crux, Max thought, and the devil answered. 'We could change that.'

She laughed. 'I'm two years older than you. That would be taking advantage of you.'

'Yes, please, madam.' They both smiled but Max didn't feel amused. She really didn't get it. Probably never would, But now wasn't the time to push it, even though it would be so easy to lean over and kiss those laughing lips of hers.

Down, boy, he warned himself. 'Seriously, Georgia. You may be older by year or two, but not in the ways of the world.' That was what he said. What he thought was, Can't you see I want all of you and I'm trying to stay away?

'Anyway,' he said, 'my aunt left me an old house overlooking Byron Bay, which she bought when she went through her arty phase. I thought I'd stay there and commute to Meeandah.

'The house is run down but if you're bored you might be interested in organising to have some work done on it. A gardener comes once a fortnight and the house itself gets springcleaned every couple of months so it will be perfectly habitable.'

She frowned. 'I appreciate your confidence in my interior decorating skills but I don't need amusement, Max, I need to rebuild my life so I can regain my independence.'

He knew she expected them to part after the twelve months, she'd told him so several times, and he'd deliberately put no pressure at all on her about his own growing feelings.

Perhaps if he spent more time with her she'd decide he was the catch of the season. What a joke. She'd confirm what he had always known that he didn't have much to offer her.

He couldn't have children and she was a great mother and should have lots of children.

He wasn't used to such negative thoughts and lack of self-confidence and if this was what falling in love did, he wasn't impressed.

He'd just have to put up with the agony in the slim chance that she'd realise they would deal very well together in the long term.

'Why don't we go for a drive on Sunday in the Hummer?' he said to change the subject. 'My poor baby hasn't had a rough-up for a few months now and Mrs White has offered to mind Elsa for a few hours.'

She glanced at him quickly and then away. 'Fine,' she replied, though she sounded surprised.

It wasn't roaring enthusiasm. She'd said fine, so he'd work on it from there.

He hadn't been out for a while and it would be interesting to see whether Georgia was a bush-bashing girl or not. Tayla certainly hadn't been.

'What are you smiling at?'

He looked up at her. 'I was thinking about the one time I took Tayla out in the Hummer and she had hysterics as soon as I turned off the main highway. She liked sitting up above all the other cars with people watching on the main road.'

'That would be the part I'd hate most.'

'Wait until you see what she can do.'

'Should I regret agreeing?'

He raised his eyebrows suggestively. 'We'll see.'

Max loved having Georgia beside him in the Hummer. They took a short drive into the hills that first day and the rough fire trail he'd chosen carried them deeper into the forest in a slow incline towards the trig point at the top of the hill.

The overhanging branches slapped the side of the vehicle and Georgia laughed with delight as they bumped and crashed their way through the bush.

'I'm impressed, Max,' she said, laughing at him as another huge frond of prickly lantana swished down the side of the paintwork. 'You really do take your baby offroad and rough her up. You're not just a show pony.'

'I'll give you show pony,' he threatened, and turned down another trail that seemed even more overgrown than the last but then cleared and opened out to a rocky outcrop overlooking the valley floor.

When Max turned off the engine, bellbirds pinged their songs in the scrub and the rustle of lizards could be heard, scuttling away from the now invaded open ground.

'You were lucky this wasn't a dead end.' Georgia gazed around in delight.

'Technically it is. But call me lucky,' he said,

and then pulled the map from the door. 'Actually, I cheated.'

'Pretty cool navigating anyway,' she said and, undid her seat belt. 'Can I get out?'

'Absolutely. Do you want a hand to climb down?'

'No.' She pretended to frown at him. 'Thank you. I'm a big girl.' Max watched her jump from the cab and he climbed out himself with a grin.

This was another side he hadn't seen of Georgia. She glowed with vitality and enthusiasm as she crunched her way across short grass and small boulders to lean, a little recklessly, he thought, over the edge.

On the other side of the canyon a waterfall fell hundreds of metres to the valley floor and the twisting sliver of a silver river at the bottom.

Max came up next to her, ostensibly to share the view but really to grab her if she overbalanced, and when she looked across at him her eyes sparkled as she took in the magnificent views.

Max smiled back indulgently at her. He was falling deeper and deeper in love with this woman every minute and he was beginning to think she wasn't as immune to him as he'd thought.

'There's nobody within miles and miles of us, is there, Max?'

'Nope,' he said. 'All this within an hour from home.'

'Elsa would love it.'

'We'll bring her next time.' Max looked forward

to more days like this. His family—if only it were really so. 'No doubt she has her mother's adventurous heart.'

'I love it. I love the Hummer. I love the bush.' She looked around eagerly. 'Thank you for bringing me today, Max. I needed a total change and this is wonderful.' She spread her arms and in doing so shifted a collection of rocks from under her foot that threw her off balance for a moment.

Max pulled her back against him before she could really grasp that she had been in danger and then she didn't know whether the thumping in her heart was from the near fall or…from being in Max's arms against his delicious chest.

Thankfully he made light of it as he righted her and shifted her to a safer position. 'Falling for me, are you, Georgia?' he said.

She could do that—despite all the reasons she shouldn't. Why wouldn't she? She felt so connected to him at this moment. Two consenting adults in the wild with no one to see what they did. Deep inside a little voice cried plaintively. Why hadn't he kissed her?

'You're a safer place to fall than over the edge,' she said lightly, hoping he'd put the breathlessness in her voice down to her near miss when, in fact, it had come from her own unexpected erotic thoughts that wouldn't go away.

'Glad you think of me as safe,' Max said dryly, but Georgia was busy with her own thoughts.

Fairly explicit, unexpected thoughts. Nymphs and satires. Naked in the bush. Max's chest.

Ants and rocks in your back... Her sensible side brought her back to earth, and Georgia turned away to hide her flaming cheeks.

What on earth had those fantasies come from? She pushed the graphic pictures from the front of her mind and searched for diversion in other appetites. 'Let's picnic here.'

'Fine.' Max's answer was short and she glanced at him. He was watching her and she could feel the blush steal up her cheeks just from looking at him so she turned away again to find Mrs White's picnic basket.

'I'll get it.' Max had the other door open. 'You find a spot to put the rug. I don't want ants in my pants.'

She laughed. They both had ants on the brain. Max came across with the basket and suddenly she was ravenous.

After the first Sunday trip when Max discovered Georgia enjoyed an adventure as much as he did, a whole new facet of their relationship opened up.

They began to take Elsa with them for excursions in the Hummer as well. They travelled along old fire trails and explored deserted gullies lined with lush tropical greenery and soaring gumtrees.

Elsa had her feet dangled in tiny tumbling streams and Max taught Georgia how to winch logs that had fallen during storms and the best way to chainsaw the heavier timber that often blocked the trails.

Max promised more trips when they moved north and the tenure at Murwillumbah grew closer.

The Byron Bay house overlooked the ocean across rolling green hills, and Georgia felt at peace there immediately.

The house was a white-painted Queenslander design with decorated gables and wrought-iron rails that marched out of sight. Two-storied, it had more wrought-iron fans that embraced the veranda posts, like the wedding cake they hadn't had.

Two of the front wide bay windows faced the not-too-distant ocean and to sit and dream over the shifting sea always made Georgia sigh with pleasure. There was even a telescope trained on the horizon to idle away time.

Her temporary posting had come through for part-time work at Meeandah Hospital and last night she'd decided that no matter how beautiful it was on the swing seat here with Elsa on her lap, she'd spent almost ten years of her life gaining experience and qualifications for a job she loved—and it was a good thing she would finally use those skills.

It was time to go back to work and the day had arrived. She just needed to get her act together.

Georgia weighed the keys to Mrs White's car in her hand and suddenly wished she didn't have to go. She'd feel differently once she was there but it was hard to leave Elsa for the first time for eight full hours.

The last four months had been necessary to rebuild her shattered confidence and learn the art of motherhood. She knew she couldn't stay in this bubble. The real world was out there and she needed to prepare herself for when this hiatus was gone.

When the year was up she and Max would part ways and that thought brought greyness into the bright sunshine of the morning. It had become harder to imagine no Max in her life, which in itself was dangerous.

Apart from when he worked, since that night she'd began sharing meals with Max, they'd rarely been apart.

They been to the beach at Byron Bay and the lighthouse and shopped at the cosmopolitan markets that sold everything from home-grown coffee-beans to the finest silk and jewellery. They'd picked herbs from Max's aunt's herb garden and lain on the lawn in the evening to see the first stars.

Yet always at the back of her mind Georgia had known it had to end.

She had to end it, because even though they'd managed to keep out of Sol's orbit for the last few months, she knew there was more trouble to come.

She would never forgive herself if anything happened to Max. Max had no idea how obsessed her ex-husband was, and when Sol actually found out she'd married Max she had no idea what he would do.

Now that she wasn't the gibbering mess she'd been after Elsa's birth, it had come home to her how unfair it was to drag Max into her troubles, and she could feel the stormclouds gathering on the horizon.

With their locum move to Meeandah, she had the opportunity to sink her teeth into obstetrics again even if it was only for a couple of weeks, and that meant she would be one step closer to independence.

Max had been wonderfully supportive about her starting work and her daughter would be settled with Mrs White in the new house for the hours she'd be away.

Her first shift since she'd become a mother herself had arrived.

She slipped back into Elsa's room one last time to check her baby was still asleep. Elsa's tiny fist was jammed against her mouth and every few seconds she'd suck gently in her sleep. Georgia knew she had to go.

When Georgia walked into Meeandah Maternity Ward she could hear the cry of a hungry baby and it brought a tiny smile to her face. She really did love being around birthing women and their babies.

Her biggest problems in her work had not been the clients or the midwives, it had been old-school, entrenched-idea doctors. Those medical officers who interfered with the natural process of birth because of their own impatience or lack of confidence in the birthing woman. Those who called a woman's labour a 'failure to progress' when often it had been a doctor's 'failure to wait'!

The nurse manager of the hospital had seemed impressed with Georgia's qualifications and experience and Georgia had felt the warmth and quality of the care and facilities from the moment she'd stepped through the doors. This hospital met the needs of their clients first and she couldn't wait to be a part of it.

For her first morning Georgia's handover report was given by another senior midwife who greeted her with delight. 'You came. I thought it was too good to be true.'

Georgia smiled and held out her hand, but the woman hugged her instead.

'I'm Karissa, and I've been trying to secure at least a week's break for a couple of months now, but staffing hadn't made that possible. With you here I can leave without feeling like I've abandoned the ship.'

Georgia looked around her and it felt so darned good to be back in a maternity unit. 'I'm just as keen to get back to work. My baby is four months old and I've left milk with our housekeeper. I hope she'll be fine.'

'I fed my son, Hamish, like that for a year when I went back to work. He managed well. We're glad to have some help here.'

'So you have someone in labour?' Georgia felt the exhilaration build.

'Yep. I'll take you in and introduce you. The rest of the ward can wait. We've only two other maternities in. The general ward staff will watch them while we have someone in labour. Most of the alternate lifestyle women here go home four hours after birth and the two mums we have staying are Caesareans births back from the base hospital.'

Georgia followed her new friend down the ward to the end of the corridor and was given a chart from the bench outside the birthing-room door.

'So let's do it.' Karissa tapped the notes. 'Mel and Tim are having their second baby. The first labour was quick and with no problems two years ago.

'Mel is due tomorrow. She began regular painful contractions at five this morning and the pains are now gradually increasing in intensity.' Karissa pointed out the graph she'd charted.

'Her waters broke at six.'

That's how it's supposed to be, Georgia thought as Elsa's wild birth came to mind. And then she thought of Max, but he was too distracting a thought when she was at work. 'It sounds great.'

'They're excited. She seems to be well established in this labour and, except for some baseline observations, I've left them pretty much to themselves to get settled in.'

Karissa knocked and pushed open the door. Mel was leaning over a bench and Tim was massaging her lower back with a rolling dolphin massager.

They both looked up briefly and smiled but withdrew their attention until after the contraction finished.

Georgia liked that. The mother needed to stay focussed. She glanced around the homey room. Floral home-made curtains, comfortable recliner rocker, beanbag and gym mat in the corner. It all made for a relaxing atmosphere.

Karissa quietly reminded her where all the emergency medical equipment was hidden behind flip-down cupboards and Georgia had been orientated to the rest of the ward a few days previously by the nurse manager.

While they waited for Mel's contraction to end, haunting instrumental music strummed from somewhere unseen, and it added to the mood in the room which was intense but focussed.

Mel sighed long and loudly and Georgia saw her shoulders drop with the release of air and the prompt of Tim's soothing stroke on her shoulder.

She stepped forward to introduce herself quietly before the next contraction hit. 'Hi. I'm Georgia. I'm taking over from Karissa. You're both very good at this, aren't you?' She smiled.

'So far it's better than little Andy's labour,' Mel said.

'Great.' Georgia picked up the foetal heart monitor. 'That's a great tummy you have there, Mel. Will it disturb your rhythm if I listen to your baby's heart rate through the next contraction, please?'

'Go ahead. We love to hear the baby.' Mel patted

her stomach. 'It is a pretty cool watermelon but I'll be glad to swap a heavy bulge for a baby.'

Georgia leaned in next to Mel and placed the finger-shaped ultrasound doppler a few inches below Mel's belly button and the clip-clop sound of Mel and Tim's baby filled the room. Everyone smiled until the next contraction started and Mel and Tim went back to work.

The baby's heart rate continued strongly and even picked up pace for most of the contraction before evening out again. Mel sighed as the contraction finished and the baby's heart rate clopped along merrily. Satisfied, Georgia stepped back and wiped the conducting jelly off Mel's abdomen.

'That's great. Baby is cruising in there. I'll leave you for a few minutes to complete the handover with Karissa and then I'll be back to do a few observations on you. Then we'll talk about your preferences for the birth.'

Georgia followed Karissa out the door and closed it behind them. They could hear the murmur of the next contraction starting.

'They're wonderful.'

'Yeah. Lucky you for a nice shift and you get to catch a baby. Come on, I'll show you the rest.' Karissa breezed into an open ward where two women sat up in bed, eating their breakfast.

'This is Leanne and Tanya, our two postnatal ladies. And this is Georgia, who is your midwife on today.'

'Good morning.' Georgia waved. 'I'll see more

of you when we've had our baby, but for the moment do you need anything in case I get tied up in the birthing room?'

'I'm fine.' Leanne waved them away with her piece of toast and Tanya smiled and shook her head.

'I'll see you later, then. You can buzz if you need someone, but otherwise just have a lazy morning and we'll catch up later.'

'Sounds good,' Leanne said around her next bite.

'Leanne likes her food,' Karissa whispered with a grin as they walked back towards the desk. 'I just wish I could put it away like she does and still stay that thin. And if you can't find Tanya, she pops out for a cigarette. She's trying to give up.'

She glanced at the clock and grimaced. 'That's about all. When Mel's ready to birth, push the red call button and one of the girls will come down from the ward to help you.'

'The on-call doctor...' Karissa grinned cheekily '...in this case your husband, can be contacted on the pager number if you need him.'

Georgia nodded and fought down the warmth that spread through her just thinking of Max. It was happening more often when she thought of him. What was wrong with her? 'What about pain relief orders if Mel wants something?'

'There is a doctor's standing order book there which spells out the options, and it is countersigned by the locums when they come the first day. I usually let the doctor know if I give any analgesia or do an internal examination so they know where the woman is in her labour in case we need them. Otherwise they will drop in before and after work.'

'Thanks,' said Georgia. 'That all seems pretty standard to any of the small hospitals I've worked at.'

Karissa picked up her bag. 'I have a feeling Max would like to be here but if you ring him don't let him push you out of the way for the birth. We can't have him begin bad habits and we catch our own babies here. But he'll let you know when he does his morning round.'

Georgia savoured the thought of having Max there for their first professional birth together. It would be lovely to share such a moment with him and until she knew what sort of back-up the general ward nurses wanted to be, the idea seemed sensible.

Karissa went on. 'It works for us. On paper, it's sad our only OB GP has retired, but in fact he rarely came for deliveries and high-risk women were shipped out anyway. If we stick to low-risk labours, I can't see why we couldn't do what we've always done and keep training midwives to be autonomous and the unit open. Fifty miles away from her family to the base hospital is a long way to send a woman to have a normal delivery.'

'I agree. It's crazy that it all depends on some number-cruncher in a distant city.'

'Don't start me on that. That way is madness, girl.' Karissa had obviously been there. 'We're just dots on the big picture.' She shrugged and yawned. 'But I've been up all night and what I vote for at the moment is going home to bed. Good luck and happy birthing.'

She pulled the drug keys from her pocket with a wry smile and handed them over. 'I'm so glad I didn't accidentally go home with the keys and have to come back.' She yawned again. 'Bye.'

CHAPTER FIVE

ALONE and in charge of a labour, Georgia thought wryly. It had been a while.

She had a quick look through the two inpatient records to check there were no medications due and why the women had chosen to have Caesarean births. Both had had babies in the breech position and their doctor had suggested they not attempt vaginal deliveries.

She reminded herself to ask Max what his stance on that question was.

She picked up Mel's chart and quickly scanned her previous labour and antenatal history, before tucking the chart under her arm and heading back to the labouring woman.

'Hi, guys. How are you going in here?'

Tim looked a little more stressed and Mel's smile had slipped. 'It's getting tough now,' Mel said through clenched teeth, and the next contraction cut off her sentence as she began to rock and moan with the force of the pains.

When the contraction had eased, Georgia quickly checked Mel's blood pressure, temperature and pulse, and then listened to the baby's heart rate through the next contraction. All observations were normal and she documented the progress in the nurse's notes.

When she'd finished she crossed to the cupboard where the large blue exercise ball was kept. Georgia rolled it across the floor to show Mel and Tim. 'Would you like to try sitting on the ball in the shower for a change, Mel?'

'I might fall off.' Mel gave it a quick glance and shook her head. 'The ball wasn't here last time.'

Georgia rolled it around in front of herself and sat down on it to show Mel. She tried to move it with her hands while sitting on it and the ball didn't budge. 'It sticks to the floor and won't roll away when you are on it, Mel. Balls are very safe.'

Mel frowned and then nodded that she understood.

Georgia went on. 'Your legs must be tired. Sitting here will straighten your back and encourage the contractions to work straight down with gravity and onto the cervical opening to make the contractions achieve as much as they can, just like the position you are in now.'

Georgia studied Mel's strained face and her instincts told her Mel would get some relief sitting for a while. 'The position you're in now has been great but you may benefit from a change of position, even if for a few minutes. It's getting tough.'

'Too right it's getting tough.' Mel glared at her husband and Georgia restrained her smile. When a woman began to express irritation towards her partner, it often meant good progress in labour.

'You could take the ball into the shower and while you sit you could direct the heat of the water onto the area giving the most pain. You can sway from side to side too—all those things will give good relief from the pain.'

Tim grinned. 'What a salesperson. Do you have shares in the company that sells birth balls?'

'Absolutely. Have a go, Tim, and tell Mel if it feels safe.'

Tim lowered himself gingerly onto the ball and never looked in danger of rolling away. 'I see what you mean about it sticking to the floor. If you don't want the ball, Mel, I might sit here to rub your back. Mine feels better already.'

That was too much for Mel. 'Get off. My turn.'

She sat, sighed into it as her back straightened, and smiled. 'Ok. Let's try the shower with this thing, then.'

Georgia wished that Max had been here to see that. Pain relief wasn't always something you had to prescribe. She went ahead and turned on the water to warm and placed the ball in the corner of the shower room.

Two rails on the wall gave Mel safe purchase as she lowered herself onto the ball and when the handheld shower was directed onto her lower abdomen where the contractions hurt most, she sighed blissfully. 'Oh, my. That is good.'

The next pain began and she pushed the nozzle close to her stomach, streaming the hot water across her abdomen. Georgia could see she'd gained relief from the change.

Georgia pulled the shower chair up behind Mel and gestured to Tim. 'If you sit behind her like this you won't get too wet and can rub her back firmly with your massager when she gets pain. Your back will get a rest, too.'

Tim settled himself and soon they were back into a rhythm.

Georgia could see they were getting close to the end of the first stage of labour and she quietly went back into the main room to ensure what she needed was ready. She toyed with the idea of phoning Max but held off until she had everything ready because sometimes the arrival of the doctor put pressure on the woman.

The baby resuscitation trolley was in the corner and she checked the oxygen and suction were both functioning, even though she didn't expect to need either.

A green-draped trolley held a kidney dish, clamps, scissors and some sponges, and she turned back the bed for Mel and her baby to lie on afterwards.

A tray rested on the bench in case Mel bled too much after the birth. It contained the IV line and infusion and drugs they might need. She glanced around and couldn't think of anything else she should prepare.

She went back into the bathroom. 'So where do you want to have your baby, Mel?'

'Don't I have to have it on the bed?'

'Not if you don't want to.' It amazed Georgia when women did not realise they had choices in birth position. 'You can use the birth stool or stand up or kneel down. It doesn't matter. Whichever you find the most comfortable.'

Mel glanced at Tim. 'How about I use the stool for the pushing and maybe move to the bed if I want to at the last minute? I remember last time and it would be good if I could just lie back with our baby after the birth.'

She looked at Tim again and remembered something. 'And I don't want the needle afterwards because I want Tim to cut the cord when it stops pulsating.'

Georgia nodded. 'That's fine. If your placenta doesn't come on its own after half an hour or you bleed heavily, you might need the needle, though.'

Mel checked with Tim and he nodded. 'That sounds OK,' he said to Mel encouragingly.

'Fine,' Mel said.

Georgia handed her a bottle of water and a straw to sip with. 'I'll have the stool ready when you want to get out of the shower.'

'Do I have to get out?'

Georgia laughed. 'Not if you don't want to.

When you get to the pushing stage, you can swap the ball for the stool in the shower.'

'Won't the doctor mind?'

'No, the doctor won't mind.' Max's voice came from behind the bathroom door and they all looked up. Georgia felt that warm pleasure she was beginning to associate with Max's presence.

His voice came again. 'Hi, Mel. I'm Max Beresford, the doctor on call. Sister can come out when she's ready and fill me in. You keep doing what you're doing.'

Georgia and Mel exchanged smiles and Georgia slipped out of the door.

Max watched her shut it behind her. 'Hello, Sister,' he said. In his mind he said, hello you gorgeous thing. His stomach dropped as she smiled up at him. She looked incredible.

Her eyes were shining with anticipation and yet her movements were calm and unhurried and she exuded an aura of confidence in the natural progression of events.

He fancied her badly. The tension on his side was building every minute that he was with her. Over the last few, amazingly wonderful weeks in Byron they had become closer than ever.

He knew she still needed recovery time, and he needed to give her that to have any chance for her to trust herself fully to a man again—and he wanted that more than anything.

She was way too vulnerable to make any physical demands on, he could tell by her body language if he even brushed against her, and no matter how much he ached to hold her and make her his, she had to be the one to initiate any change in that.

He had to protect himself too because all he could see on her side was appreciation of the safe harbour he provided and he was becoming more fascinated every day.

Even knowing she would be at work today was distracting but worth the opportunity to see her during the day. He hadn't been able to stay away once he'd known that it was Georgia's first morning back at work.

She was looking at him with that tiny frown he wanted to smooth away with his fingers, and he pulled himself back into the present. She expected him to say something, not stand there like a goose. 'So here I am. Were you going to call me at all?'

She looked at him quizzically. 'Yes, Doctor.'

Maybe she wasn't sure if he was serious so he smiled to reassure her.

'Mel sounds fine. I'm here before I go into the rooms for my day patients. I've read your notes and you're obviously happy with her progress and condition. Do you want me to say hello to her or just leave it until later?'

'Would you mind popping your head in to say hi now? I don't think she'll be long anyway, and it's better than meeting when the baby is here.'

Before Max could even open the door they heard Mel's voice. 'Georgia-a-a.'

Georgia stepped back into the bathroom and rested her hand on Mel's shoulder. 'It's OK. What's happening?'

'In the middle of that pain I wanted to push, but the feeling has gone now.'

'That's fine. Each pain will probably give you that feeling for a longer time and then it will come to the stage when you won't be able to do anything but push.'

Mel nodded.

Georgia went on. 'It's all good.'

Mel chewed her lip. 'I remember I hated this part last time.'

'That's OK. You might have been scared because your body is taking over. Don't hate it. Work with it and listen to your body.'

'I'm trying.'

'You're doing amazingly well.' Max's quiet voice came from the door.

'You can come in,' Mel said with half a smile in the pause between contractions. 'I really don't care if the world's in here and at least you can help me if I need it.'

They could hear the smile in Max's voice. 'Which you won't as Georgia is there and you're all doing so well. I won't come in unless you or Sister call me.'

The pains increased their intensity and soon Mel was pushing gently with each urge. The next minute she looked up at Tim and glared at him. 'I want to move. Get me out of the bathroom.'

That was a good sign. Georgia smiled as Tim almost fell over in his hurry to do what Mel asked. They stood and she moved between pains towards the bed. Mel looked up once as she passed Max and nodded to him.

'Hi, Doctor,' she said briefly.

By the time she'd eased herself back on the bed her baby was almost ready to be born, and Tim had paled to an interesting shade of alabaster.

'That's the way to do it, nice and slow.' Georgia helped Mel lean back onto the beanbag and slipped her gloves on.

Max stood back and watched Georgia. She had it all under control, brilliantly. He'd suspected she would be a great midwife and the last few minutes had proved that.

Mel's next pain came and with her steady breathing, the baby's head crowned and then extended, until only the shoulders remained to be born.

When the first shoulder came through, Georgia guided Tim's hands down and encouraged him to lift his own baby up onto Mel's chest as he was born.

Max stared at the sight of a loving father's hands lifting his son onto his wife's breasts, and the pain seared him unexpectedly, like a blow torch in his chest.

He would never do that for his own child. He would probably never share such a look as Mel and Tim shared at that moment.

'Oh my goodness,' Tim said, as he stared down

at his baby. 'It's a boy. I've got another son! My Billy.' He swooped down to kiss Mel. She laughed up at him and they both had their hands on their new son.

'There you go. Eight thirty-one a.m.' Georgia checked the clock and then she looked at Max.

He smiled back at her but there was such a wealth of sadness behind his eyes that her breath caught and she wanted to comfort him for something she didn't understand.

Then the look was gone as if it had never been. Maybe she had been mistaken and he was just tired.

Max moved to the baby and placed his stethoscope on the baby's back to listen to his chest as he lay against his mother. He stepped back and nodded.

'Baby sounds great. Congratulations, Mel and Tim.'

Georgia watched his gentle handling of baby and realised she knew so little of this man who was legally her husband and here they were together at such a special event and yet she still didn't know what he was thinking.

Georgia glanced down at the thick shiny umbilical cord and suddenly a tiny gush of blood indicated probable separation from the uterus. They were ready to complete the final stage of labour.

If the placenta had sheared off from the uterine wall then it certainly wouldn't have a pulse and Tim could cut the cord.

Georgia curved her fingers around the cord and gently squeezed the thick rope. 'The cord has stopped pulsating, Mel. Is it OK for Tim to cut the cord now?'

Mel looked up. 'Yes, that's fine.' She smiled at Georgia. 'Isn't our son beautiful?'

'You are a very handsome man, Master Billy,' she said to the baby, and then returned her attention to the job at hand.

'I'm just sealing his umbilical cord with this little clamp and pinching another section a few inches down so Tim can cut between the two clamps.' She looked up as she held out the scissors. 'You ready, Tim?'

Tim nodded and took the scissors to saw away at the cord until it was severed. 'Either the scissors are blunt or it's pretty tough.'

They all laughed when the job was done and a few seconds later the third stage was complete.

'No damage,' Georgia said after a quick check down below, and she lifted out the disposable sheet from beneath Mel and tucked the warm blanket over her chest and the baby.

Max wandered over to the bench to start writing in the patient notes and Georgia checked Mel's abdomen for a contracted uterus once more before pulling the blanket down and joining him.

Georgia frowned and checked again. Mel's uterus was soft and spongy and not the hard ball she had expected. She lifted back the sheets and a sudden column of blood spread into a widening pool that seeped away underneath Mel onto the bed.

The blood didn't just trickle, it flowed heavily in

a serious postpartum haemorrhage that needed immediate treatment.

'Max,' Georgia said, and his head flicked up immediately at the tone of her voice. He crossed over to the bed and Georgia leant over and pressed the red button for help. Max already being there was a godsend, but they might need extra hands.

Georgia's palm had gone straight to Mel's abdomen again to rub the top of her uterus externally and make it clamp down on the bleeding. Max's hand came in over hers.

'I've got it.' He rubbed Mel more firmly.

'The uterus has no tone at all. Get me cannulas for IV access and I'll slip them in.'

Georgia grabbed the tray from the bench and slid it onto the shelf beside the labour bed.

Max took one of Mel's hands and slid the tourniquet Georgia handed him over her wrist. 'Have to pop in a couple of needles so we can get a drip up. Sorry, sweetheart.'

Georgia picked up the injection tray she'd had prepared with the declined injection in it. 'You get the needle now, Mel.'

Mel nodded. 'I feel a little woozy.'

Georgia glanced at Max before speaking to Tim. 'Gently pull two of her pillows out, Tim, so Mel can have her head lower.' Tim moved the pillows and grew paler by the second as he watched the puddle of blood that filled the space on the bed below Mel's waist.

'Then can you rub Mel's tummy here.' Georgia

took one of his hands and guided him to where the top of Mel's uterus lay just above her umbilicus after the birth.

'This feels like a squashy grapefruit and it should feel like a big hard lemon.'

She looked at Mel, who was clutching her baby with one hand as she tried to breathe calmly through her nose. 'You won't like Tim much for it but it is very important he rubs your tummy fairly firmly until the uterus contracts and stops the bleeding.'

She turned to Max. 'OK if I give the first Syntocinon intramuscularly? I had it ready in case.'

'Sure. Then check the placenta. Maybe there is a bit left behind that's stopping her uterus from contracting properly.' Max concentrated on finding Mel's veins before she lost too much blood. Soon the lack of blood volume would make her veins collapse and it would be more difficult to find the blood vessel he needed.

Georgia explained to Tim, 'I need to check the placenta to see there is none missing. Sometimes a small piece of placenta can stay behind and stop the uterus from fully clamping down on the rich blood vessel bed that it's detached from.'

The nurses from the ward appeared and froze at the door, as if they didn't want to come in. 'I'm Flo,' said one, and the other just stared worriedly at the blood.

Georgia smiled at them. 'Come in, Flo. It's OK. Maybe you could take over from Tim so he can help Mel hold the baby.'

Flo nodded and hurried to do as she'd been asked.

Georgia pointed at the tray and said to the second nurse, 'Could you draw up four ampoules of the Syntocinon and put it into that flask for Doctor, please? That will help stop the bleeding. Then put another saline flask up to run as fast as it can through the other cannula to replace at least the volume of fluid Mel has lost.'

The nurse nodded and hastened to her tasks, obviously relieved that it was something she understood how to do.

Tim cradled his son and Georgia checked the placenta and then stripped off her gloves to check Mel's observations. Max had the drip up as soon as it was loaded.

Still the haemorrhage continued and Max frowned as he looked across at Georgia. 'Vital signs?'

Georgia didn't like the persistence of this bleed and she was very glad Max had come when he had. 'Her BP has fallen to eighty on forty and pulse rate is up to one thirty. I've some ergot here.'

'Thanks. I'll push it IV and see what we get.'

'Mel?' Tim's voice startled them as he leaned over his wife. Mel's face was ashen and her eyelids flickered but didn't open when Tim called out.

Max had injected the drug and now he frowned as no immediate response was noted. 'I'll have to manually compress the uterus,' Max said. Thankfully, when he did bunch Mel's uterus between his hands the bleeding slowed, though as soon as he removed his hand it started again.

'Oxygen,' Max said at the same time as Georgia passed him to reach the flip-down cupboards with the resuscitation equipment. She slipped the mask over Mel's face and tilted the whole bed so that Mel's feet were higher than her head.

'I may need the Prostin F2 alpha,' Max said quietly, and Georgia nodded and moved to prepare the syringe.

Not often used, the last drug was injected straight into the muscle of the uterus, which meant Max compressed Mel's uterus against one hand and injected the medication with the other.

Within less than a minute the gushing blood slowed to a trickle and Georgia and Max looked at each other with ill-concealed relief.

'Tricky,' Max said.

'Very, but that's done it.' Georgia breathed out with the reprieve and after checking Mel's blood pressure even allowed herself a small smile.

Mel moaned and her eyes flickered open as Tim sagged with relief.

Max checked Mel's abdomen again and her uterus finally remained well contracted. Max nodded and looked at Georgia. 'Better.'

'Thank you,' he said to Flo, and he smiled to include the other nurse, who blushed and backed away. Then Max looked at his wife. 'Well done, Georgia.'

He leant down and spoke to Mel's abdomen. 'Now, why did you do that?'

The tension lightened in the room and Mel roused enough to say in a weak voice, 'What happened?'

Tim sighed with relief and then suddenly paled further, sighed and sagged sideways.

'Grab the baby,' Max called to Flo, who scooped Tim's son from his arms as Tim fell back in a dead faint. Max caught the new dad easily under the arms before he hit the floor, and dragged him into a chair.

Max looked down at the ashen Tim. 'Just to top it off, poor guy.'

'Never a dull moment,' Georgia said, as she carried a damp facecloth across to Tim, who stirred groggily as the blood returned to his brain.

By the time a sheepish Tim was sitting upright, Mel had recovered some of the colour in her face as well.

Max jotted down the sequence of events with times and then crossed the room to speak to Tim and Mel. 'Unfortunately we probably will never know why your uterus decided not to contract after birth.'

'Mel's BP is back to ninety on fifty and her pulse is one twenty,' Georgia said.

Max nodded and spoke to Tim. 'Mel's compensating for the lower volume of blood she has circulating now, but childbearing women have extra safeguards for the risk of bleeding after birth. We'll check what her actual red cell levels are and think about blood transfusion or not and discuss it later.'

He smiled that smile Georgia really did love. 'Everyone in the room has a pulse of one twenty at the moment but it's all settling now. Mel's uterus is firm and behaving itself and the bleeding has stopped.'

He spoke to Georgia. 'We'll run the drip over four hours to make sure it stays that way and keep her in this room for a while so we can keep an eye on her to ensure it doesn't start again. But it shouldn't.'

Mel spoke faintly from the bed. 'So much for not having a needle. That was a bad choice.'

Max shook his head. 'Not so. Don't lay blame on anything in particular. Lots of people decline the needle after birth and though it statistically increases risk, it didn't cause what happened.'

Max paused to let the words sink in. 'Unless you have a history of bleeding! Now you have that history...' he shrugged ruefully '...I think your choice is limited for the future.'

Bravo, Max. Georgia wished she could clap because she knew a lot of medical officers who would have ground Mel down for her choice. She would tell him so tonight. In fact, she couldn't wait until dinner tonight and the chance for their first real discussion about a specialty of medicine they both obviously loved.

Baby Billy nudged at his mother and Georgia smiled. 'Would you like a hand to put your son to the breast? During breastfeeding more hormones are released, which will help prevent further bleeding as well.'

When Billy was settled at the breast, Georgia and Max left the new parents to enjoy their son in peace after the traumatic events following the birth.

Max slipped his arm briefly around Georgia's shoulders and hugged her before he dropped his arm to his side again. 'We're a good team. That could have been much worse if the F2 alpha hadn't worked or you hadn't been prepared.' Max smiled down at Georgia and she nodded.

'I was glad you'd dropped in when the floodgates opened. It's always tricky to do everything at once when things go only slightly unplanned, let alone a full-blown PPH. I wouldn't have enjoyed the stress while I waited for you.'

Max's eyes softened. 'Is it still good to be back at work when you have occasions like that?'

Georgia looked at him and nodded without any doubt. 'When it all turns out as well as that did then, yes, of course. And the birth was lovely.'

His face clouded again and she put her hand on his arm. 'What's wrong?'

He smiled and she wondered if it was forced. 'Nothing. I was very proud of you, my wife, in there. But now I'll have to go to work and crunch some numbers around until you call me again.'

He patted her shoulder and just before he moved off he said, 'Do ring me. Any excuse to get out of the office is gratefully accepted.'

'Perhaps you could come back at lunchtime and check on Mel and share my sandwiches.'

'Sounds like a plan.' He smiled and waved and she watched him go.

He'd been a pleasure to work with and as cool as ice in an emergency. But, then, she'd known that since Elsa's birth.

She was trying to ignore the fact that her heart had given a jump when she'd first heard his voice, and just watching him talk to Mel had made her so proud to think that for the moment, at least, he was her man.

She gave herself a little mental shake. She needed to think more about her work and less about Max.

That night at dinner it seemed the floodgates of work discussion opened. They'd never really discussed much about Max's work but it was as if he'd finally decided he could talk to Georgia and she would not only understand but be deeply interested and have much to offer him in response.

'I had no idea how much I missed the face-to-face obstetrics that I grew away from in administration.'

'How could you not notice you'd left a clinical role?' Georgia listened with her chin on her hands and watched the play of emotions cross Max's handsome face. How had she come to be with this man? His kindness to her seemed to have no limits.

'I started teaching.' He shrugged. 'And that always moves you back a pace as you encourage students to gain skills and be safe. The only way to impart that knowledge is to let them do it—which meant I didn't.

'That access to students meant people were always asking about change and why things were done in a certain way. Soon I was the person advocating change and fighting against the old school of habit.'

She smiled. He would be a good teacher. 'That must have been satisfying.'

'In its way it was,' he said with a twitch of his lips, 'but that pushed me further away from the births and into the boardrooms and medical committee meetings. Before I knew it, funding had become the big issue.'

She wouldn't like that herself. 'You must have been good at creating change?'

'Maybe, but it is paradoxical that the more I see of grass-roots obstetrics the more I want to be part of it again.'

She could listen to him all night. She'd never had this. As an only child she'd never had a sister or brother she'd been able to really relate to and she'd never been close to Tayla.

Her loving parents had died together when she had just left her teens—too young to have really understood her mother yet old enough to see that true love was a worthwhile goal.

Her marriage, after the initial honeymoon period, had never included an equal partnership so any conversations had been dominated and directed by Sol.

With Max she felt she could dispute, digress or

downright disagree, and her contribution would be appreciated. He must have felt the same because he stood up and held out his hand.

'Come and sit with me for a while on the veranda. We'll look over the ocean and check out the stars. It is a beautiful night.'

She took his hand and the feel of his fingers around hers as he helped her up made her realise she had never felt so relaxed and cared for by a man who had no expectations of her.

CHAPTER SIX

THEY rose and crossed the room and strolled out through the French doors to the veranda. A soft breeze blew tendrils of hair across Georgia's cheek and she felt Max's gaze on her as she sat down on the swing seat. He sat next to her and his strong thigh brushed hers as they swung.

Georgia took a sip from her glass and tried to retrieve the light mood they'd shared in the dining room.

The focus had shifted suddenly so that she was aware of Max's weight against her and the subtle scent of his aftershave even with the breeze carrying scents from the garden her way.

She remembered those crazy fantasies she'd had on the mountaintop and shifted a little on the seat.

She cleared her throat. 'Meeandah Hospital is certainly grass roots. You might change your mind when you've had ten nights' broken sleep in a row from callouts.'

Max spread one arm to encompass the vista and

the other he dropped around her shoulders. 'A hospital like we have here has fewer than one hundred and fifty births a year. That leaves me two hundred nights with sleep at least—not counting the quick births in the night that I'm told about in the morning.'

What a dream life as far as she was concerned. Imagine living here, Elsa growing up in this wonderful environment, Max as a true companion and lover, plus the best of doctors to work with. They were damned attractive thoughts but Max could never settle here.

'Somewhere like this is a big step down,' Georgia said as she thought of the high-powered position he'd held in the city, and even the subtle state-wide ramifications of what he achieved now, along with his visits to the hospital. His position was important to the whole scheme of obstetrics in New South Wales.

Max looked across at her. 'Could you be happy working in a facility like this?'

'Of course.' Couldn't he tell? She glanced around them at the idyllic lushness of the garden and the endless sky, and thought of the birth she had already been privileged to share. 'If the health system will sustain it, I'd stay here for ever.'

Georgia exhaled a long blissful sigh and looked across at him. 'This is what I love to do. Before I worked at Lower Mountains Base, I had my own home-birth practice, but nowadays I couldn't make that kind of availability commitment with Elsa.'

'Why is that?'

She loved it that Max seemed so interested. 'I need the framework of other midwives around me and this sort of situation is the nearest I can get to the ideal world.'

Max sat back. 'I would never have imagined this sleepy town could be an ideal world.'

She sighed. 'For you it wouldn't be. You'd miss not having the city to call on for amusement.' As she said the words, disappointment washed over her. Of course she was being unrealistic.

That was sad but true. Max would move on and she might even think about staying here when the time came for them to part, if she could be safe. Suddenly she didn't want to think about the time when Max had moved on.

Max closed his eyes and felt her words slice into him. They hurt. When had he been bored in the last four months? When had he wanted to be anywhere but coming home to Georgia?

'Do you know so little of me that you imagine that? Do you think me so needy of the bright lights?' Sometimes he despaired he'd ever have a hope with this woman. She didn't even try to understand him.

He sighed and watched her reflect back over what she'd said, but judging by her expression she still didn't get it.

'How could I know more about you?' she said. 'You don't exactly talk about yourself. Apart from the last few weeks, I'd barely seen you except for night relief from Elsa.'

He supposed it was true, though to his mind she seemed to be everywhere. When they had rare time to talk his choice would be to hear about her, not himself.

If that was the price for her to really see him then maybe it was time he began to pay. 'What do you want to know?'

She laughed and he wanted to kiss her—not talk about himself. Her infectious chuckle had been there since Elsa's birth and he treasured these moments more each day.

She poked him gently with her elbow. 'Do you realise how dangerous it is for a man to offer to tell all?'

He tilted his head. 'I asked what you wanted to know—I didn't promise I would tell you.'

'Now you are being mysterious.'

And you are delicious. He swung the seat gently and she was carried with him back and forth. She wasn't in his arms but it was better than nothing. 'I'm not intentionally mysterious.'

'So start with Tayla.' Georgia folded her hands. 'How did you meet her and what made you think you would be happy together?'

Max shook his head. 'Why do women always start with another woman?'

'Fine.' She shrugged. 'What do you want to tell me, then?'

His gaze locked with hers. 'I'd rather tell you that

I have enjoyed the last four months with you more than any I can remember.'

Georgia's eyebrows rose in disbelief. 'Sure,' she said. 'It must have been a hoot for you. You enjoyed being woken up by a colicky baby ten times a night and having a grumpy, sleep-deprived housemate to live with.' Why on earth would he?

'Absolutely.' The tilt of his lips confirmed that he had only pleasant memories and though he spoke quietly, his tone of voice indicated it was the truth. 'I became acquainted with Elsa and she's gorgeous, like her mother.'

Georgia tilted her head. 'Same temperament, you mean?'

Max nodded. 'She's determined and independent, yes.'

'Ah.' She had him. 'So living with me is like living with a baby with colic. I can see why you'd be attracted.'

They were teasing each other and she was beginning to enjoy it too much. This was far too dangerous for her peace of mind and she tried to steer the topic away into more general waters. Maybe he did have an agenda with her after all or he'd managed to beam in on one of her fantasies.

'It is a glorious night,' she said.

Max wouldn't be diverted. 'I appreciated each and every vision of you at night since Elsa was born.'

Georgia thought back over the range of short cotton nighties and men's T-shirts and boxer shorts she'd worn, with her hair a mess. Not much to admire there.

He hadn't finished and his voice brushed her skin with his breath as he turned to face her. 'And I was privileged to see your hair wild and loose and the real you without the public face of composure that keeps me at arm's length so very efficiently.'

This was serious stuff and she wasn't sure where it had come from. The mood on the veranda had deepened to one of charged closeness and she couldn't help softening against him. Georgia forced her arms to cross to block out the intimacy. To block it out because suddenly she wanted to reach across the seat and hug him for seeing a real person and not an object to own, like Sol had.

Obviously Max recognised the moment too and she must have given away more than she'd intended because she saw his surprise and the next thing he'd acted on the impulse she'd denied herself.

Very slowly but with intent his hand slid up her spine to the back of her head to hold her in place and then he leaned across and kissed her gently.

His lips savoured hers in a long slow exploration and his breath was warm as it mingled with hers.

Suddenly boneless, she sighed into him because it felt so damn wonderful and right and what she desperately wanted, and just for a moment she followed Max's lead as she felt her fingers tighten on his shirt and she pushed her hand against him back and forth just to feel the hard heat of his chest.

But this wasn't right. She forced her fingers open

and then his shirt slipped away, just like the moment had to. The last thing Max needed was a clinging vine, he'd said himself he admired her independence, and she pushed the feelings away along with his chest because she already owed this man too much.

She could not get involved with Max. Not while Sol's presence in her life hung over her.

She sat back and, Max being Max, he let her go. Which was a shame but the right thing to do.

For her to offer something that wasn't really there wouldn't be fair to Max and she was beginning to think if she let down the barriers and allowed him into her own rapidly beating heart, she would never find herself when she left.

'Thank you, kind sir,' was all she said, and she leaned forward to stand up. 'I think I'll check on Elsa.'

Max's hand caught her wrist and the strength in his fingers halted her rising.

'I'm sorry if I embarrassed you.'

She looked at him, at his strong jawline and then his warm golden eyes, and she said quietly, 'You didn't embarrass me, Max.'

'Then why are you running away?' His voice, too, was barely audible.

She breathed in and the faintest tinge of his after-shave remained on her skin. 'You had a nice life before I came along.'

He laughed cynically. 'I nearly married the wrong woman before you came along. You saved me from a fate worse than death. I've been very happy with you, Georgia.'

'Tayla offered what you wanted, Max. A free life without the dramas of a family. Elsa and I have plenty of dramas. You haven't married the right woman yet. I'm only the stopgap.'

Just when he thought they might have made progress, he'd lost her. He could see it. 'What if it doesn't feel that way to me?'

'Then you would be thinking with another part of your body, not your brain.'

Ouch. She definitely wasn't ready to change their relationship. He'd like to get his hands on that ex-husband of hers and throttle him. He was beginning to think there was more to his nastiness than she'd said. He let go of her wrist and she stood up.

She nodded and left almost at a run, and Max gazed out over the veranda. He'd scared her—but for a moment there he'd thought she was on the same wavelength as he.

Max watched a tiny meteorite arc down towards the ocean and disappear before it reached the water, a bit like the opportunity that had just passed him.

He could wait. He would have to. He would wait until she was secure in herself.

He guessed that wasn't going to happen until she knew Elsa was safe from her father, but he hoped he, Max, wasn't too old to enjoy it by then. It was so damn hard to keep his hands off her.

He wondered what he could do differently to dis-
sipate the awkwardness he'd created between them.

For someone who had never had a problem with
come-hither lines, he'd botched it badly. No doubt
the difference being this time he was emotionally
involved and becoming more so every second.

The feel of her lips against his had been as
poignant as he'd anticipated. The need to feel the
rest of her against him rose like Mount Warning in
the distance and just as appropriately named. He
would have to be patient.

Georgia gently pushed open the door to Elsa's room
and moved to stand beside the cot. Her tiny daughter
lay in a shaft of moonlight and her rosy cheeks
glowed with health as she sucked her lip gently in
her sleep.

Why couldn't she and Elsa have the wonderful
life she had begun to suspect Max could offer her?

Because even now Max might be hurt when the
time came that she had to leave with Elsa because
from what he'd said tonight, he could certainly
become attached to her daughter.

Max had told her he'd planned not to have
children with Tayla so the same reasons were still
there. Yet here she was with a baby that was
anything but easy at times. The upheaval in Max's
life had been caused by a child he wasn't even the
father of.

Apart from recently, the poor man hadn't even

left the house except for work because of her and Elsa. Even Mrs White saw that.

But she, Georgia, was a mess and Max didn't deserve that or the danger she would bring in the future.

Max had no idea how much trouble Sol could be and although she really needed to leave now, before she did any more damage, she couldn't. It wouldn't be safe to leave while she was still vulnerable to Sol with Elsa so young.

She glanced down at her defenceless daughter again and reality slapped her with the obvious she had begun to forget. What was she doing even contemplating her own happiness before the safety of Elsa?

As a mother she should be concentrating on her baby and setting up her future life, not fantasising about a man she could bring to ruin by association.

Her problems were not Max's, though he obviously was beginning to think they were. They needed to avoid the type of comments and moves he'd made tonight or it was all going to become much harder. She would never be free to take on emotional issues with any man and Max didn't deserve that.

On Tuesday morning Georgia stayed out of the kitchen until Max had gone to work.

Cowardly, but she hadn't been able to face him, because some time in the night she had discovered that with all the reasons for not staying with Max the one that loomed largest was the fact that she'd fallen irresponsibly in love with him.

She was a fool. Though this time, at least, she had fallen for a worthy man. Which was all the more reason not to drag him into the danger she knew was ahead.

What was becoming obvious was that Max wanted more, wanted to move their relationship onto a whole new plane, and she had too much baggage to drag him down with her.

She'd just have to be careful to keep him safe by maintaining her distance. And she'd make sure Max did, too.

That night at dinner, sitting across from Max, she tried really hard not to glance out to the swing seat on the veranda and think of Max's kiss at this time last night.

From the way he kept glancing at her, she had the feeling Max was remembering too.

'How's your sawdust?' Max said conversationally.

'Fine,' Georgia said, as she tried to rationalise with herself about how she was doing the right thing to block Max out. Then his words sank in.

'What did you say?'

'We're both chewing away diligently but I had to look again to see what I was actually eating. I think we should both accept that while it is very nice to kiss it causes problems in our day-to-day world for the moment.'

Georgia could feel the heat in her cheeks but she

was glad Max had had the courage to clear the air before she'd had to.

'I agree,' she said, which was pretty lame but that was the best she could do at the moment. She forced herself to meet his eyes. 'Thank you, Max, for understanding.'

'You're welcome. Now let's talk of something else. You didn't miss any obstetrics at the hospital today so I hope you have someone to play midwife with tomorrow when you go in for your next shift.'

She followed his lead gratefully. 'You did say your statistics pointed to one birth every two days.'

'I'm infallible. I know you enjoyed your first day.'

Georgia thought back to her first shift and smiled. 'They even paid me to have fun and brush up on my emergency obsterics. And it worked well because I was home by three in the afternoon and still had a few hours to feed and bath Elsa before you came home. Mrs White is looking forward to tomorrow with her.'

'So you are happy to be back at work?'

'As long as Elsa is fine, I love it. I should at least be able to do next week and if possible a short stint full time to allow Karissa her holidays, which would give me a good basis to refresh my skills for the future.'

He raised on eyebrow in disbelief. 'I don't think your skills need much refreshing, Georgia. I'm extremely comfortable that you would cope with anything.'

Max's approval meant a lot. She had been surprised how at ease she'd felt at Meeandah, but Max's presence had been that extra insurance she'd needed to make it easier. 'Thank you, Max.'

She avoided looking at the swing again and decided she did feel a little easier already.

'So tell me about your day at home,' Max said. 'What exciting things did I miss?'

He even looked interested. 'Big news. Elsa opens and shuts her hands now.' Georgia smiled reminiscently. 'You wouldn't think something so small would captivate both of us but she lay there for ages, watching her fingers open and shut, and I had to watch, too.'

Max smiled. 'I'll have to ask her to show me in the morning. When you go to work she shares her breakfast with me and I read the paper to her.'

'She'd like that.' Not many men would do that for a child that wasn't even his own. Georgia fell more in love with him than ever and went back to eating her sawdust to avoid his eyes.

At Meeandah hospital Georgia had agreed to three staggered morning shifts in the first week.

The idea had been to see how Elsa and Mrs White got along and how Georgia coped with being away from her daughter for the first time since Elsa's birth.

Her second shift was uneventful.

Max came in and discharged Mel to go home. He'd issued a prescription for double-strength iron tablets to increase Mel's red blood cell count because she hadn't wanted the blood transfusion Max had offered after her haemorrhage.

'Don't expect to do much except breastfeed Billy for the first two weeks to keep building up your milk supply,' Georgia said.

Max stood beside her to wave them off with a few cautionary words for Mel. 'Your low blood count will slow your lactation so Billy will be extra-demanding and you will be tired.'

Mel shrugged. 'I'm too excited to be going home to worry about that. Tim's going to do everything except feed. He's got three weeks off work.'

'Good man,' Georgia said, and she slanted a sideways glance at Max. 'Max is excellent with Elsa, too.' The two women smiled at each other as Tim looked proudly down at his son tucked under his arm.

Max shook his hand. 'Good luck, mate. At least the men outnumber the women in your house.'

Tim grinned and carried Billy carefully to the car and strapped him into his new baby seat next to his brother, Andy.

Both Caesarean patients, Leanne and Tanya, had decided to go home too, and after Max left the ward Georgia worked in the medical end of the hospital.

She enjoyed the challenge to brush up on the medications and treatments she didn't deal with in obstetrics. It also gave her a chance to get to know the other nurses she might have to call on in the future.

She gathered that Flo and her colleague didn't feel as comfortable as they'd like at the obstetric end and Georgia could see why if they only went there for the last minutes of labour or in emergencies.

'When it's quiet, would you be interested in practising some obstetric emergency procedures, just so you would have more of an idea what we might want you to do?'

'That sounds great.' Flo was in her sixties, round and energetic with a host of grandchildren she loved to talk about. Georgia loved the way she and Gerry, the other nurse, were keen to update their skills and be as helpful as they could.

Gerry was tall and thin with a mournful face, but her wicked sense of humour appeared at the strangest times. Both women's interest in learning about obstetric emergencies encouraged Georgia to go on. 'If you find it helpful, we could do a different emergency each shift that I'm on.'

Later that day, when all the patients were resting, Georgia went through the postpartum haemorrhage tray with Flo and Gerry.

'I thought we'd start with the emergency we've already had.' She couldn't help thinking of the way Max had so competently directed the emergency. No doubt it was still very fresh in the minds of Gerry and Flo as well. So she was pretty sure she'd have their attention.

'With a postpartum haemorrhage the excessive blood loss can happen for different reasons. You can have a sudden heavy bleed, like we had with

Mel the other day, where the woman bleeds quickly and things need to happen fast before she goes into shock from blood loss.'

Flo nodded. 'Shock is when the body makes changes to ensure enough blood goes to the brain isn't it?'

'Yep. Like Mel's pulse rate going up because her heart has to circulate fewer blood cells faster to get enough oxygen to her brain. That's why the patient feels faint. If a person faints, they automatically lower their head and make gravity at least push blood to their brain. That's why I raised the foot of the bed for Mel's feet to be higher than her head.'

Georgia saw that they had the concept and moved on. 'Or you can have a woman go back to her room and bleed quietly in a steady trickle until she is in just as much trouble. They're usually the ones who buzz because they feel faint when they get up to go to the toilet.'

'We had a lady do that…' Gerry nodded soulfully '…at my training hospital back in the bad old days. When we went to make her bed she'd trickled steadily under the covers over a couple of hours and we nearly had a fit when we went to help her get up. She nearly died.'

Flo's mouth formed an 'O' of surprise. 'So that's why we check postnatal women for the first four hours, just like a post-operative patient gets checked in Recovery.'

Georgia nodded. 'But remember it's not normal for

a healthy woman to do that. The body has mechanisms to prevent it, but some women don't know they are in trouble. Basic observation is very important. Rapid emergency treatment can save lives, and that's where having everything ready to go is so important.'

Georgia removed the haemorrhage tray from the cupboard. 'Let's have a look at the tray we have here. You obviously need your IV fluids, a tourniquet, your cannulas to insert into the vein for access, and connection tubing for administering the fluids. You both remember Doctor connecting these to Mel. Then there are the drugs that can help with contracting the uterus.'

Georgia held up a sheet of paper in a plastic sleeve. 'This is the order and dose of the drugs you would need, and that can be very helpful if no one has time to repeat what they asked for.'

Gerry snorted. 'Typical. I wish I'd known that was there, even though I did manage to get them all in order.'

Gerry acknowledged she'd worried the previous day and Georgia was glad they were talking about it again. She realised Gerry had probably been rehashing the events and needed this discussion to debrief after Monday's excitement.

'An emergency is a stressful time. Extra reminders are always helpful. These trays save everyone from running to find different things, too.'

Flo nodded enthusiastically. 'Boy, do I know what you mean. Every emergency I've ever been in I seem to be hunting for things other people want.'

Georgia smiled. 'The most important thing to get is help. Even the kitchen lady to write down what you gave and when and what steps you've taken can be good if you are short-staffed. That's why the pad and pen are here.'

She held up a pen with a long cord attaching it to the pad. 'We all find it difficult to get the time drugs were given exactly right even if we record an event immediately afterwards.

'The beauty of recording events at the time is that we can make fine adjustments when we go over our treatment and actions and review later.'

Gerry snapped her fingers in enlightenment. 'Is that what a critical review is? I thought it was when you were critical of what people did or when they'd done something wrong.'

'No. It's feedback to make the next situation run even more smoothly. Max is going to sit down with us later today and we'll go over it together and see if we missed anything.'

'I don't think there was anything anyone could have done better,' Gerry said dryly. 'I thought you guys were amazing.'

'We were a team and you and Flo were an important part of that. I think you both were pretty wonderful, too.'

On Thursday Max was called into Maternity just as he was about to go home for the evening meal and he didn't return until after Georgia had gone to bed. They'd had a sick baby with congenital heart problems and Max had waited for MIRA to arrive to stabilise and take the baby to Newcastle Hospital with her mother.

He'd rung and let Georgia know he'd be very late and she'd sat in the dining room by herself and had then gone to bed early. She couldn't believe how much she'd missed his company for that one evening.

She had geared her day off to when Max came home. Things she'd planned to tell him. An article she'd thought he might be interested in. And the extra time she'd taken with her appearance.

These were all warning signs that Max was assuming a larger part of her life than she'd promised herself she'd let him be.

CHAPTER SEVEN

ON GEORGIA'S third morning shift the day dawned cold and damp, with thick fog that engulfed the mountain and the road on the way to work. Georgia had left fifteen minutes early to be on the safe side and still only arrived as the clock hit seven.

Minutes after the night staff had departed a young woman hobbled miserably into the ward with her friend. She stood at the nurses' desk with her hand cupped protectively around her small belly and her lips pressed tightly together.

Georgia came back from the medical end of the hospital at the sound of the buzzer and something about the young woman's stance sent alarm bells ringing.

'Can I help you?' The young woman nodded but didn't speak.

'She's having contractions,' Her friend said, 'and you need to stop them.'

Georgia blinked. OK. This was different. 'I'm Georgia, the midwife. Would you both like to come through to the observation room and we'll see what's going on? Then I can ring the doctor.'

The spokeswoman nodded. 'I'm Shannon and this is my friend, Del. She's got eight weeks to go.'

Georgia glanced at the silent Del and her heart rate picked up. They'd have to fly her out if she was in labour—they couldn't handle a baby that size here. Even the base hospital wouldn't take her at that gestation.

Shannon went on. 'She's having twins.'

Georgia's eyebrows rose. They'd have to fly her out urgently, which would be interesting with the fog. A twin pregnancy was even more likely to progress to a premature delivery.

Del froze as she went to sit on the bed and she grabbed Georgia's hand and squeezed it as her contraction mounted. Georgia slid her other hand down to gently feel Del's belly through her shirt, and it felt rock hard against her fingers.

Georgia reached for the buzzer and pressed for assistance. She glanced at Shannon and although Shannon looked scared, at least she could talk. Del certainly wouldn't be talking for a minute. 'How long has Del been having contractions?'

'It took us an hour to get here and an hour before that.'

Two hours shouldn't be too advanced in labour for a first baby, Georgia thought hopefully. 'Is this your first pregnancy, Del?'

Shannon came to the rescue when all Del did was

shake her head. 'Her third. The last one took two hours.'

Georgia smiled at Shannon. 'I'm glad you came with her.' She looked at Del. 'You're not much of a talker, then, Del?'

Before Del could answer, if she was going to, a slightly breathless Flo arrived.

Georgia smiled at her. 'Today we're going to study the premature labour tray.'

Flo grinned and headed for the cupboard. She reached in and put the tray on the bench. 'I hope it comes with instructions.'

'You'd better ring Doctor, first, on his mobile. Tell him thirty-two-week twins in labour. He'll come straight in.'

Flo's mouth formed her favourite 'O' and she pulled the phone book across.

Georgia helped Del to lie on the bed and connected the monitors to her stomach. 'These belts hold on the listeners that hear your babies' heart rates and record your contractions at the same time. In your case we have two listeners for two babies' hearts.'

Del nodded and winced as the next contraction started. Georgia could hear Flo's brief conversation with Max.

She looked up. 'Ask him if I can give the first dose of nifedipine as her contractions are three minutes apart.'

Flo nodded back. 'He heard you and said give the first dose. He'll be here before the next one is due.'

She hung up and came back across to Georgia. 'You want some observations done?'

'Please. I need to check Del's antenatal records as well.'

Shannon was the only one with a shoulder-bag and Georgia directed her next enquiry to her.

'Have you got Del's antenatal card?'

'She doesn't have one. She's only been the once because the doctor said she'd have to go to Brisbane to have her babies. She didn't want to do that so she never went back to him.'

Georgia's heart sank at the lack of antenatal care and information now available. 'Where were you going to have your babies, Del?'

Del looked at Shannon. Shannon answered. 'Here.'

Thirty-two-week twins here and no antenatal care. Meeandah was good but not that good.

Georgia rummaged through the tray and removed a strip of tablets and two spoons. 'We want to stop your labour Del. I'll crush this tablet between two teaspoons and you have to put it under your tongue until it dissolves. It's actually a blood-pressure tablet that works on the muscles of the blood vessels but it relaxes uterine muscles as well.

'The plan is that you have fewer contractions the more tablets you have.' And the doctor arrives soon after, Georgia thought hopefully. 'Do you under-stand?'

Del nodded. Georgia looked at Shannon and lowered her voice. 'Does Del talk at all?'

'Sometimes if she has to, but she finds it hard.'

'That's OK, Del. As long as you understand and let me know if you need to know more—OK? And as long as Shannon stays.' She grinned at Del's friend.

Del nodded and opened her mouth and Georgia thought she was going to speak. She held her breath but Del only waited for the crushed tablet before closing her mouth again.

'When the doctor comes, he'll want to examine you to see if your cervix is opening. That makes a difference to what we do next. OK?'

Del nodded.

'We'll probably give you an injection to help your babies' lungs mature in case they are born too soon.'

Del nodded and Georgia found herself nodding too. It all began to feel like a farce with all the head-bobbing.

Georgia selected the cortisone injection from the tray and set it aside for Max to decide on. They'd need to liaise with whatever referral hospital had beds for premature twins but MIRA would set up the conference call between the parties as soon as Max rang them.

MIRA, standing for Mobile Infant Retrieval Australia, would fly mum and babies wherever they needed to go with expert personnel—as long as the mist lifted and they could land.

'Can you give Del's doctor's name to Flo and she'll get him to fax what info he has to us here?'

she asked Shannon. Shannon nodded and followed Flo out.

Max arrived sooner than was prudent, considering the road conditions, and Georgia was glad to see him safe as well as have access to his assistance.

'This is Del.'

'Hi, Del. I'm Max. I'm the doctor. Georgia says you're in premature labour. You must be pretty scared at what's going on.'

Del looked around for Shannon and Georgia held off answering for her to see if Del would speak.

She nodded.

Georgia did Shannon's job. 'Del's not much of a talker. She's having contractions three minutes apart, third pregnancy, quick labours. One antenatal visit, one ultrasound at eighteen weeks. They're faxing it through as soon as they open the surgery, I guess.'

'Good stuff.' He held his hands up. 'May I feel your tummy, please, Del?'

Georgia nodded along with Del and then realised what she'd done. She was going mad.

She left Max to jot down what she'd found so far and by the time she'd finished Max was ready to examine the patient.

Afterwards he pulled the chair up beside the bed to talk to Del. Georgia leaned out the door and called Shannon to come back in.

'Shannon is spokesperson and she does a great job. It might be worthwhile waiting for her.'

Max raised his eyebrows and looked at Del. 'Is that what you want, Del?'

Del nodded vehemently but she didn't say anything.

Max sat back and Shannon hurried back in with Flo at her heels.

Georgia took Flo aside. 'Can you switch both humidcribs on in the storeroom? Probably won't need them but if it looks like we will then we'll move them to the power points outside the door. Just leave them where they are for now as long as they are warming.'

Flo nodded and left.

Max had introduced himself to Shannon and then spoke to Del. 'You're four centimetres dilated and your babies need to be looked after by paediatricians when they are born.' He paused to let his words sink in.

'That means they're too little to be looked after here at Meeandah. In fact, they're too little to be looked after at the base hospital so they'll have to go to Newcastle, if they have the neonatal beds free, or Sydney.'

Del's eyes filled with tears and Max rubbed her wrist in sympathy. 'I know it's scary to think of going a long way away but you have to for your babies' safety. When your babies are bigger, you will be able to come back here for them to finish growing up.'

Del nodded and looked at Shannon, who asked

the question. 'How long before she would come back?'

'That depends how Del's babies grow and the treatment they have when they are born.'

Max went on, 'It is much better for babies to be transferred while they are still inside your tummy. It takes a lot of very sophisticated equipment to make an environment close to as good as your uterus is for your babies. We need to get you to a big hospital before your labour gets any further along. Do you understand?'

Shannon, Georgia and Del all nodded.

Max smiled at the three noddies. 'I'll be speaking to a doctor who will find where and when you'll be going and when I know I'll come back and tell you.

'In the meantime, Georgia is going to give you two more tablets twenty minutes apart. Maybe later also an injection that will help the babies lungs mature for when they are born. Let Georgia know if you think your labour is getting stronger, OK?'

'Than' 'ou.' Del's quiet voice stopped Georgia as she turned away. So Del could speak. Trust Max to have elicited a response when she couldn't. Were any women immune to the man?

'You're welcome, Del.' He gave the young girl one of his special smiles and Del smiled mistily back.

Max stood up and examined the CTG tracing. 'Your contractions have slowed a little to five-minutely so the first dose of drug is working. Georgia will give you another tablet now.'

He looked up at Georgia. 'I'll be in the office on the phone if you need me.'

In the next twenty minutes Del's contractions slowed to ten-minutely but they didn't stop. Flo had been outside to see if the fog had lifted but the mountain still lay shrouded.

Georgia sought Max out as he finished the admission letter for whichever hospital would finally take her.

'Del's contractions are strong and very regular, sitting at ten minutes apart.'

He spread his hands. 'There's a chance one of the outlying Sydney hospitals may take her, otherwise she may have to go on to Canberra.'

'If they don't decide soon, she'll get her wish and deliver here.' Max seemed very calm considering they might have premature twins on their hands. 'We'll send her out by road ambulance to the base hospital until the fixed-wing aircraft can land.'

Georgia frowned. She'd tried that. 'They refused her.'

'With the airfields shut, they've OK'd it now. They said they'd even send the escort. But if she's in strong labour they won't take her on the plane either so she'll have to go somewhere.'

Georgia smiled. Max had really done some ringing around. 'You wanted the joys of rural obstetrics.'

He grinned at her. 'Aren't you having fun?'

'The more the merrier.'

Max looked at her. 'You may have spoken too

soon.' The screech of tyres could be heard coming hard round the bend into the hospital and they looked at each other as another screech heralded the arrival of someone in a great hurry.

A tall, bearded man rushed in, his eyes panicky with emotion. 'Help us. My wife, Susie, is in the car, and she's having the baby right now.'

Georgia tapped Max's arm. 'You go. I'll get the emergency kit and a warm blanket and meet you there.' Max nodded and jogged after the man.

Georgia hurried to collect the small tray, a warm blanket and infant rug from the hot box and a wheelchair in case they could move the woman to a more comfortable place for delivery.

By the time Georgia arrived they needed the warm blanket for the baby and the cord clamp and scissors.

The husband was calmer now that he wasn't alone to cope and it was a very relieved family that moved into the ward to ensure all was well.

Susie clutched her baby to her as if she didn't know where he'd come from.

'It's all a shock but you did beautifully,' Max said with a smile. 'Your son didn't mind in the least being born in the car. He'll probably grow up to be a rally driver.'

Flo stuck her head into the room. 'There's a phone call for you, Doctor.' Max nodded to indicate he was returning to the other room, and Georgia had to smile at his mode of communication. Very appropriate for Del.

Susie shuddered. 'Not if he drives like his father did on the way here. The fog made it a nightmare.'

'Susie's blood pressure is up,' Gerry said mournfully.

'Mine would be, too,' Georgia said with a smile. 'Perhaps you could just check it again in fifteen minutes, please. I'll go back to Del if you settle everyone and maybe offer a cup of tea in here.'

'Sure.' Gerry was happy to have something to do with all the excitement. 'Flo's had all the fun this morning,' she said.

Fifteen minutes later the ambulance arrived to take Del to the base hospital until the fog lifted, and Georgia only just finished all the transfer papers in time.

Max put the phone down. 'They don't want the steroids given or any more nifedipine.'

'Do they want us to check her cervical dilatation before she leaves?' Usually patients were assessed to ensure delivery wasn't imminent or likely to occur during the transport period.

'None of those things,' Max said with a frown. 'I queried it but the consultant was adamant.'

'Things change all the time. Must be a new study out that I haven't heard of,' Georgia said, but it did seem strange to her as well.

Georgia signed and printed her name and packaged her letter and Max's letter to the consultant stating what they'd done to go with Del.

A midwife from the base hospital had arrived as

escort, which meant Georgia didn't have to call anyone in to cover for her.

Suddenly the ward was quiet. All they had to do was clean up and prepare for the next person to come in.

After all the excitement it was a bit of an anticlimax and she wished Max could stay and have a coffee with her but she didn't ask because it felt needy.

He waved and left and instead Flo and Gerry helped Georgia restock the trays.

'This tray thing works pretty well.' Flo repacked with satisfaction.

'I wonder which one we get to use next,' Gerry said gloomily, and Georgia laughed.

When Max walked in after work that night, Georgia had Elsa on a rug on the floor in the lounge. Elsa was stretched out on her tummy, kicking her legs with her nappy off as if trying to swim.

For Max, seeing mother and daughter so relaxed in his home, squeezed his heart so hard it was almost chest pain.

He despaired of ever being a part of their closeness. He should just enjoy this now because since the other night Georgia had created a distance between them he could feel growing every day.

At this moment she was laughing at the fierce expression on Elsa's face as she tried to propel herself forward.

Georgia glanced up at him with her face alight

some flowing shirt with a deeper neckline than usual that highlighted the smoothness of her long throat.

They'd skipped pre-dinner drinks on the veranda because of Elsa's late settling and now he was separated by the width of the table. He just wanted to touch her.

The sky grew inky outside, with clouds obscuring the stars, and Mrs White had retired for the night, leaving dinner in the kitchen.

Before he'd come home Max had rung through to see which receiving hospital Del had ended up in and how the babies were. Mother and the newborn twins were stable and settled. The one bad piece of news had been the consultant who had received them—Sol Winton.

Max still debated if Georgia should be told because he suspected the news would upset her. He knew her ex-husband had given Georgia an emotionally hard time as well as making her severely depressed.

During the last four months Max had seen no signs of paranoia or depression—and anyone with a colicky baby could easily plead depression—so Winton had obviously had some hidden agenda.

Still, she was away from him now and, theoretically, hearing about his hospital shouldn't upset her too much.

He dragged his thoughts away from his quandary and caught Georgia in the middle of a half-hidden yawn. She even looked cute when she yawned.

'You must be tired,' he said. 'It takes a while to get used to shifts again.'

She tucked her hand away from her mouth ruefully. 'Not really. Do I look it?' In fact, she looked a little crestfallen at his observation, and Max grinned.

'You look positively haggard, darling,' he drawled, and Georgia blinked before she realised he was joking.

'Teaser.' She shook her head at him and changed the subject. 'How was the rest of your day?'

Max tilted his head. 'Actually, you look stunning.' He watched her frown at him but he was darned if he shouldn't say it when he meant it.

He moved on when she grimaced at him. 'Now, what was your question? My day? After our exciting morning?'

He ticked off his fingers. 'Del's twin girls were born at midday and all are well. They weighed over twelve hundred grams each so I don't know where she was hiding that weight. The girls are breathing for themselves and may start tube feeds tomorrow.'

'That's wonderful.'

Before Georgia could ask more he went on hoping to change to another topic. 'Even bigger news is that Tayla and my brother, Paul, have decided to get married. We're invited to the wedding but guess who is not invited to be bridesmaid?'

'Me?' Georgia tried to look sad.

He shook his head sadly. 'I know you must be dreadfully disappointed.'

ent dilemma now. He didn't want to upset Georgia by bringing the subject up again but she needed to know he was happy to talk about how she felt if she wished.

If she gave him the option. The silence lengthened and he guessed they were both going to pretend nothing was wrong.

Georgia felt gutted. She wasn't even sure Max knew it was Sol's hospital.

She tried to quell the pictures that rose unbidden into her mind. It's OK, she told herself. The connection with Del wasn't so bad. Was it?

Sol would have to be the receiving consultant on duty to have had any contact with Del. Even then the registrar would probably have been the one to read the nurse's notes.

There really wasn't much chance Sol would track them down, and she doubted Del would speak much about Meeandah except to nod.

Georgia just wished she hadn't been the one to sign and print her name on the nurse's transfer letter—along with Max's. She still signed her maiden name because of the rigmarole of changing names through the nurse's registration board so Sol would recognise it.

'We have the weekend before us. What can we do to put a smile on your face?'

Georgia looked up at him blankly.

'Would you like to go somewhere? For the weekend?' This time it had been Max to change the

subject and she was glad because her own brain
still felt sluggish with shock.

The idea of hiding away from the world appealed
to Georgia greatly. 'Let's go away. Drive bush roads
for the weekend. Follow where the tracks take us.'

Nobody would find them and she would be able
to push the thoughts of Sol far into the back of her
mind again. She'd just begun to feel settled and
happy but now the secure rock Max had built for her
had crumbled away with only one obstetric transfer
to Sol's hospital. Her response in itself was dis-
heartening.

'Go camping, you mean?' Max was looking at
her as if to judge how serious she was.

The idea promised sanctuary, Georgia thought,
clutching at anything to divert her mind away from
the past. 'No phones, no people—just the bush and
us.'

'I think it's a great idea to take some picnic
supplies and get offroad,' Max said cautiously, and
she looked up in surprise. She'd thought he would
have jumped at the chance to camp out.

He went on. 'How about we run back into the
coast at night to sleep with civilised showers and
comfortable beds? Away from the mosquitoes, for
Elsa's sake.'

The urgency to hide loomed larger than comfort
for Georgia. 'Elsa will be fine. I thought you
enjoyed roughing it.'

'Logistically it's a little easier for me to camp
than you and Elsa. If you don't fancy the coast

there are fabulous mountain retreats in the Lamington National Park. We could slip across into Queensland and go up into the mountains and make log fires in the retreats at night when Elsa goes to bed.'

She sighed with relief. They could still go. 'That would be wonderful, Max. Could we?'

'Sure.' He stood to collect their plates. 'We can decide where we'll go after dinner. I'll go online later and check it all out. I do have friends up that way who own a lodge.'

She watched him head for the kitchen. She normally would have jumped up to help him. He was solicitous and she guessed he must have connected the hospitals, too.

She felt like someone had dropped a boulder on her smooth life when she wasn't looking. To get away this weekend would at least give her time to get her thoughts together without jumping at every sound.

She hugged herself and the feel of her arms reminded her how it had felt when Max had first agreed to look after her. That first day that Sol had seen Elsa.

She stood up, walked to the window and gazed out into the inky blackness. Far away on the ocean a container ship rode the horizon. Alone and undefended it could still look after itself.

She wasn't ready to do the same and she didn't know what to do for the best.

What if Max was in danger, too?

Max entered the room and placed the dishes on the table, not trying to be quiet. He expected her to turn from the window but she didn't seem to hear him return.

When he touched her on the shoulder she flinched so violently that his hand pulled back and his own pulse rate soared.

'Hey.' He stepped closer now that she knew he was there and slid his arm around her shoulder. When she didn't pull away he turned her into his chest and encircled her. She was shaking and his chest tightened. He would protect them both with his last breath.

'You only need to tell me how you feel and I'll share it with you,' he said and teased her gently. 'You're not alone and I'm deeply offended you think you are.'

'I'm sorry, Max.' She sniffed into his shirt and his hand slid up and brushed the hair out of her eyes. Her expression of deep foreboding twisted his stomach.

He wanted to snatch up Georgia and her daughter and carry them away from any chance of Sol finding them and that was when he began to realise she would never be free until the Sol issue was resolved.

'Even if it is only for a year, I am your husband. Who better to protect you? I may seem a flipperty sort of fellow but I do have hidden strengths.'

'You don't seem flipperty at all. You're wonderful.' She glanced at his muscled arms and gave a twisted smile. 'Your strength isn't hidden and I don't deserve your patience with my bogeyman.'

'Cut it out, Georgia. If we are anything, we are friends.' He lifted her chin. 'Isn't that right?'

'Yes.' She nodded and buried her face back into his shirt.

'So friends trust each other and your worries are my worries. But we do need to communicate. It is very hard to help you when you shut me out.'

'I know.' She straightened and he hugged her one last time before he forced himself to let her go.

'Come and eat. Then we'll talk. Unless we feed all this food to the dog, Mrs White will find out we didn't enjoy her hard labour.'

'I couldn't eat a thing.'

Max stared down at her and she looked so forlorn and lost that his heart ached to ease her pain.

He leant forward again and kissed her gently on the lips with all the tenderness she inspired in him. She sighed against him and didn't pull away, and when he drew back she turned her face towards him and leaned up to kiss him back. He forced back the desire to pull her into his arms and really kiss her so she could forget the man that stood between them.

'I'm scared, Max.' Georgia leant her head on his chest again.

'I know, darling.' He had felt her tremble beneath his lips when their lips had met. He couldn't see how one man could inspire such dread but Georgia obviously could.

'Hold me,' she whispered.

He'd imagined holding her in his arms many times, but not for this reason. Poor baby. 'Any time you want, Georgia. You only have to give me a sign.' He gathered her in and she rested her cheek against him. Then she turned to look up at him.

When she closed her eyes and invited another kiss, he could no more stem his response than stop the waves on the beach he could hear in the distance.

He cupped her chin and traced the pure lines of her face with his mouth as he'd longed to do since Monday night. Her skin felt like velvet and glowed like cream, and he wanted to taste both. He brushed her eyebrows with his lips and then the tip of her nose before settling on her lips in homecoming.

She tasted divine, as he'd known she would, and he searched deeper, always waiting in case she pulled away, but she responded with a hunger that smouldered like his own. Her response tore at him so strongly it was difficult to remember he had to hold back.

When he raised his lips from hers to stand back, she murmured in denial, still with her eyes closed, so he leaned forward and took her mouth again in a kiss that left them both breathless and stunned by the connection between them.

They stood, wrapped in each other's arms, breathing as one, and for Max it was as if he were standing under the full brunt of a waterfall, and he could no more hold back the water than he could hold back the urge to carry Georgia to his bed and make her his.

'I need you to take me, Max.' Her words echoed his own desire, but the need in her voice inflamed him as nothing else could have. When he lifted her into his arms her head lay back to expose the soft column of her throat, and he brushed his face against the tender skin there to inhale the perfume of her skin before straightening.

She sighed into him with such softness and warmth he pulled her against his body and whisked her up the stairs before either of them came to their senses.

When he placed her gently on his bed she reached up for him without hesitation, but a brief moment of sanity stilled his hand before she tugged at him and he lowered himself down beside her.

'Are you sure?'

'Kiss me, Max.'

He'd dreamed many times that he would hold her in his arms and protect her from the world. Yet though he wanted to make her his, he needed to ensure her own feelings of self-belief were restored. That was more important than anything. For him this was right, but what of her?

For Georgia, all intrusion from Sol had vanished with the safety of Max around her. Somewhere in the distance her brain disagreed, but the last time Max had lowered his mouth she'd felt the leashed force of his need and that had made her forget. She wanted that again. She pulled him closer and answered the call without permission from any inner voice.

She slaked his hunger with her own and when, peripherally, she felt her clothing move and then his bare skin against hers, she could no more stop her response than she could stop her own heart beating.

His chest was rock hard against her and flattened her breasts gloriously against him. Her fingers skimmed the V of hair on his belly and she exulted in his caressing hands as she caressed him.

It wasn't enough.

Suddenly there was no time for niceties, neither did she want them. She wanted Max.

She wanted Max over her, in her, joined to her, and she wanted him now. She'd never felt a need as strong and overpowering as this before, but the need was ancient and she demanded his response to wipe out all that had come before.

She could feel Max try to slow the pace but deep inside her a dark fear despaired that something would prevent their union, that some sinister force would tear them apart, and the very least she wanted was this consummation to make her whole again.

Max rose above her and she stared up at him. His strong throat soared above her and his chiselled features were outlined in the darkened room. His golden eyes stared down at her with all the fierce need for possession she'd stoked in him with her own need.

Their eyes locked and she reached up to savour the bulge of taut muscles in his arms as he lowered himself gently against her. Her eyes widened as he entered her, slowly, intimately questing, deeper and deeper, until his whispered name escaped her.

He stared down and the adoration in his face made the tears slip beneath her lids and then he withdrew until she protested. He smiled and entered her again. Slow and steady and deep until again she moaned his name and only then did he quicken the pace.

Georgia clutched at his back to stay with him and they rose and fell together in a long slow erotic dance that drove everything out of their minds except the feel of each other in union.

When it was over they lay together, her head on his chest and his arm encircling her as if he'd never let her go.

She knew the moment he slept and she turned her head and kissed his chest. 'I don't want to hurt you,' she whispered. 'Maybe there is hope. We'll see.'

Through the night they joined again, but this time in a slow dance of discovery that scaled the heights again in a different way until much later they slept, entwined.

This time Max lay awake until the morning when he watched her wake up to see if he had been a fool.

He'd promised he would keep her safe and what had he done at the first temptation but taken her like a caveman bearing his prize? He hadn't been able to resist and now he scanned her precious face for any sign of regret.

At least he couldn't make her pregnant. He

winced with the pain that reflection brought, but the pain was nothing to the thought of losing Georgia.

She'd been mind-blowing and incredible but even in the midst of their magical storm he'd feared she'd only wanted to escape from her memories and that he'd taken advantage of her when he should have waited for the right time.

Now he was afraid he had created more dilemmas for her, which was the last thing he had intended.

He knew he loved this woman above all things but he also accepted he had to create an out for her if that was what she needed. No matter that it would rip out his heart to put distance between them again—a greater risk was destroying any chance of their future.

Not when he'd found the one woman he'd never known had been out there. He could not taint that again with her regret.

'Good morning?' He couldn't help the question mark at the end of his greeting and inside his head a devil mocked him.

'Good morning, Max.' Georgia chewed her lip.

Max's stomach plummeted and he forced himself to smile. He'd known she would regret it.

'There is something I need to tell you,' she said and his gut twisted.

At least she hadn't said she regretted the night, yet. Max brushed her cheek with his hand and then reached for her fingers to hold in his. 'So tell me.'

She searched his face and what she saw there encouraged her to go on. 'When I moved back in with Sol to protect my friend...' She paused and closed her eyes for a second as if compelling the words to come, 'He overpowered me and forced himself on me in a horrific night I thought would never end... And that is how Elsa was conceived.' She shook her head at her own stupidity. 'I hadn't foreseen him doing that.'

Max's voice was low with shock and how he would have done things differently if he'd known. He didn't know what to say. 'Did you go to the police?'

'Who would believe me when he was my husband? He's respected and I was supposed to have paranoia. They'd say that I went back to him and cried rape. I was shattered and the whole situation was a nightmare.'

Max felt the words hammer into his brain and unconsciously he squeezed her hand. He could tell there was more. 'Go on.'

'I ensured my friend was safe from him and I left. I vowed no man would ever do that to me again. I never wanted to think about sex again. Last night all that changed. I needed you and you answered my need.' She smiled crookedly. 'Handsomely. You've taught me to trust my instincts again.

'I'm sorry if you think I used you but suddenly I needed you to wipe the slate clean and show me that making love is just that. And you showed me how it should be and I can never thank you enough for restoring my faith and my self-esteem. But last night was not the beginning for us.'

Max felt as if his heart was breaking for her courage. 'My poor darling.'

He didn't know how she'd stayed as sane and strong as she had with such a man. Max ached to come across Sol in some dark alley some time and make amends for Georgia.

He had trouble getting the words out past his regret that he hadn't known her then. 'Not all men are like that.'

She shook her head as if to say that wasn't her concern. 'I'm scared for you, Max.'

How could she worry about him at a time like this? 'Don't be, because I swear to you now, that man will never hurt you again. If he tries, he will have me to deal with.'

He wanted to tell her that he truly loved her with all his heart and soul, but to pressure her now with that would be selfish. He needed to step back and lay more groundwork before he went there.

Instead he said, 'Let's still go away for the weekend. Forget all this and just relax together with Elsa.'

'Could we?' He saw the way she looked up eagerly.

He nodded. 'We could pack and be out of here by ten, if you still want to.'

Her eyes met his. 'I'd like that.'

Down the hallway the baby cried and the chance of more discussion was lost as she slipped from his bed. She pulled on his robe and he knew she would go to her room with Elsa and not return. He knew from the way she didn't even look back as she left.

He knew what he was fighting for and he was even more determined. He would woo her as she deserved.

CHAPTER NINE

THEY drove to the mountains and the spectacular scenery lifted Georgia's spirits in a way she couldn't believe, especially now that there was even more to think about.

It seemed Max was going to make it easy for her by not discussing last night. Her body glowed every time she thought of those stolen hours—but that's what they had been. Stolen and not to be repeated.

Max had no idea what they were up against. Their time together had been an amazing escape from the reality and despair that just hearing Sol's name had again left her with.

Thankfully, it seemed that Max would bide his time and perhaps, if a miracle occurred, maybe some time in the future they could travel that road.

At least Max had helped her understand that when someone cared for you, making love was just that—making love. Love in a way both parties felt more together—not less!

But though their intimate time had strengthened

her acceptance of how much she loved Max, it had also given her more reason to leave.

Max desired her, there was no doubt about that, but this morning's relaxed dismissal of their night together had made her wonder if he had the capacity to love or just make love.

Maybe it was better if Max didn't love her. Safer for everyone.

They stopped many times along the way north to Queensland. The all-terrain vehicle crawled along hardly used bush trails, showed them great vistas over rainforests and let them enjoy escarpments decked with eagles and graced with tumbling waterfalls that smashed down onto boulders far below.

Lunch was another picnic packed by Mrs White, which they had beside a cold mountain stream, and afternoon tea saw them back on the coast and an hour and a half east of their destination.

They drove through the Lamington National Park three thousand feet up to the rainforest retreat and Max was greeted like a long-lost friend.

The owners, Paddy and Morgan, had even arranged for their daughter, Trish, to sit with Elsa in the room later that evening while Max and Georgia enjoyed their dinner.

The suite Max had secured, instead of the two single rooms she'd expected, made her pause at the door, and Max's hand rested on the small of her back as he waited for her to say something.

They could see over the canopy of trees from the

window but it was the two big canopied beds that dominated her vision.

'The suite is lovely, but it seems strange they didn't have two single rooms.'

'I didn't ask for singles, Georgia. We're a family, even though you and I may not sleep together tonight.' Max met her eyes unswervingly. 'I thought you'd be more secure if I was right here with you and Elsa.'

When she didn't answer he went on. 'Despite last night, you can trust me. As you can see, we have two doubles and there's a cot for Elsa.'

He shrugged and changed tack. 'Actually, I did it for myself. The nightmares have been a problem and tonight I'll have you to protect me.'

Georgia glared at him. She wouldn't make a fuss. It would be ridiculous after what had passed between them, but she'd thought he'd understood. 'I hope Elsa keeps you awake all night.'

He shrugged. 'She's done that before.'

This wasn't happening. Last night had been a mistake that she couldn't regret but had no plans to repeat. 'Any designs you have on me will not come to fruition, Max.'

'I'll have you know that I am saving myself.' Max averted his face primly.

As if. 'You're not a virgin any more, Max.' Georgia couldn't help the reluctant grin he'd dragged from her, despite her best efforts to remain cross.

'That was only my body,' he said solemnly.

'You…are…mad.'

'I'm crazy with it all right,' he said, and this time no humour lit his face. She was a fool. He really had only thought of her, but before she could apologise for doubting him, Elsa stirred.

'I'll see you down in the lobby where the maps are displayed,' he said, and she filled the silence with movement as Max slipped out the door.

He'd told her to trust him and she'd never had cause to disbelieve him. That was the baggage Sol had left her with, and she wasn't going to start not trusting Max.

Elsa settled quickly after her feed, and Trish arrived with her own dinner on a plate.

After a brief discussion over what to do if Elsa woke up, Georgia completed her make-up and brushed her hair again. Strangely nervous, she went to meet Max downstairs.

As she came down the stairs the way his gaze travelled over her made her glad that she had spent the extra few minutes on her appearance and her nerves dissipated like smoke from the chimney.

This was Max. Tall, gorgeous Max, with his incredible body and amazing hands and amazing mouth that just thinking about sent waves of colour to her cheeks. Max, her refuge, her husband, even if it was only for a year, and the man who was looking at her as if she were the one person he'd ever wait for.

Max smiled that wonderful smile of his and held

out his hand, and when she put her fingers in his she realised how right it had been to get away.

'Welcome to our first real date,' he said as the waiter showed them through the doors to a private table in a bay-windowed alcove.

She smiled. After all they'd been through. 'For first-timers we've had our moments of interest together,' she said, and the thought of last night tingled her skin in a pink glow.

'That's no excuse not to catch up on the stuff we missed out on,' Max said, and she saw the flutes of champagne and laughed.

A long-stemmed red rose lay across her setting and she glanced up at the waiter with a smile. 'Does everyone get a rose when they come here?'

'Only those on their first date,' the waiter said, and smiled. The man pulled out her chair and Georgia sat and looked around at the restaurant as Max chose the wine for the meal.

The room was long, with several bay windows overlooking the valley below that disappeared in the darkening twilight.

A log fire crackled in a central fireplace and added pleasant warmth without overheating the room. Her throat felt warm but she knew the heat was from something else.

Exposed wooden beams crossed the ceiling with relics from the roaring days of the pioneers, but there was nothing rough about the service or the fine china.

The waiter left after ensuring they were happy,

and Max raised his glass to hers in a toast. 'To a tranquil weekend.'

She'd drink to that. 'Utopia.' They clinked the delicate crystal and she sighed blissfully. 'What a gorgeous place. You've obviously been here before.'

Max glanced around and his face softened. 'My aunt loved this restaurant. I used to come here at least once during my holidays with her.'

There was a note in his voice she'd never heard before. 'Tell me about your childhood and parents.'

He put his glass down and grimaced. 'Now, that's a boring story.'

She frowned at him and he held up his hand. 'But I did say I'd answer questions.'

He smiled whimsically. 'My father was a worthy man, an excellent surgeon with very little sense of humour, who retired one month before he died of a heart attack.'

Georgia stretched her hand across the table and touched his in sympathy where his fingers lay against the tablecloth. He looked at her briefly and then looked away.

'My mother now lives in America with her new husband and apparently is reasonably happy.'

It sounded emotionless and she couldn't help being disappointed by his distance.

'Try a little harder, Max,' she said. Though what did she expect when she was the one creating distance all the time?

He sighed laboriously and then went on. 'My parents had very little in common with each other, or me, but led a very civilised life together. My brother and I spent a lot of years at boarding school.

'Fortunately, I spent a lot of my holidays with my mother's sister, who owned the house in Byron, while Paul stayed home and became even more worthy.'

His face softened and his beautiful mouth curved. 'My Aunt Beatrice I could talk about for hours.'

'Please, do,' she said softly, aching for the boy who had obviously been lost in boarding school and at a family that hadn't known how to love.

Maybe that was why he had chosen Tayla and had such low expectations of marriage.

'Beatrice was a widow. Her husband died early in their marriage, which was very considerate of him. I'm sure she was happier doing as she liked. She was an Amazon of a woman who adored bright colours with the black she said she wore for mourning.'

He grinned at the memories. 'She could put colours together. Black and gold stripes, black and emerald spots, black and hot pink, sometimes all of them at once, and always adorned with lots of beads.'

He shook his head. 'She'd have sunflowers growing in her garden and they were all over the house in vases. She'd sing the blues in this gravelly voice that would raise gooseflesh on my arms.'

He glanced around the room as if seeing memories from the past. 'She loved to sculpt and paint and you've seen all the luminous stars she glued onto the ceilings in the house at Byron. She loved the stars.'

'Beatrice sounds wonderful.' But best of all was the affection she could see for his aunt on Max's face. He'd loved his aunt. There was hope yet.

'I adored her. She could be incredibly selfish but that appealed to me too—so much more interesting than worthy. She listened to me and told me she loved my company, when my parents couldn't wait to send me back to school.'

His face became expressionless. 'She nursed me when I was sick in my late teens and made me see how much I had to live for.'

She didn't like the sound of that illness. 'In what way were you sick, Max?'

'Hodgkin's disease. I had it for two years and stayed in Byron with her. She drove me to Brisbane for treatment.'

Georgia knew Hodgkin's could kill and that it struck down adolescents and young adults, more often young men. 'You were one of the lucky ones, then?'

'They say I'm cured.' He nodded but there was the sadness behind his eyes she'd seen before. Suddenly she realised why he'd never seemed to want children—the radiotherapy would make that unlikely. She didn't comment because he didn't, though her heart ached for him. But it all began to make sense.

'How did your aunt die?'

'Beatrice? In her sleep. Peacefully. After a big dinner party one night five years ago. She loved company and food—the higher in cholesterol the better.'

He glanced down at the béchamel sauce on his steak and smiled wryly. 'Enough about me. Try to enjoy your meal without my sob story to put you off.'

Conversation turned desultory and time passed.

With dessert Max had questions of his own. She could tell he was happy to not talk about himself any more. 'So, did you have a perfect childhood?'

She shrugged, reluctant to lose the mood of warm companionship. 'My parents were very much in love, and instilled in me that love is worth waiting for. But they died when I was young and an only child.'

'Who brought you up?'

'Harry. Tayla's mother was very like Tayla. She wasn't a warm woman and Tayla resented my presence in her family.

'Harry tried to make up for it because he is a kind and decent man, but that only made Tayla worse. Harry's always been able to see Tayla's faults and he protected me to some extent. I tried not to be too much of a problem.

'Tayla's mother died when I was eighteen and Harry and Tayla are my only relatives, except for my darling Elsa.'

His hand came across the table and squeezed

hers for a moment where she held the glass. 'And your darling husband, Max.'

'That's true.' She smiled at him and then glanced at the grandfather clock against the wall. 'That was a wonderful dinner. Thank you, Max.'

Max looked at the clock, too. 'It's still early. Let's take a stroll before we go up. There's a night walk to the glow-worm forest that only takes about half an hour each way. You could check on Elsa first and then join me.'

'Glow-worms?'

'Yes,' he said, and his voice dropped low and portentous, like a 1950s horror film. 'The larvae of the fungus gnat.'

She burst out laughing. 'Imagine having that pearl of information at your fingertips.'

'You have no idea what information I have.' Max steepled his hands. 'Hurry and you will learn more.'

'Yes, sir.' She saluted and turned for the stairs.

She chuckled all the way up to the room. If it was fine with Morgan's daughter, seeking glow-worms sounded like a lovely way to end the evening.

Max watched her walk away. The curve of her hips, the column of her neck under her swinging hair. So close and yet so far.

He wasn't going to make the same mistake twice. He'd just have to make sure he didn't touch her because there was no doubt they had ignition problems he couldn't be sure he could control.

She was back within minutes, pulling her woollen wrap around her shoulders. 'Elsa hasn't stirred and Trish is halfway through a movie she wants to see the end. So we are free for an hour. Show me the worms.'

'I love it when you talk dirty to me,' he said with a deadpan face.

'I'm a very earthy woman.' she quipped back, and they smiled at each other.

It was blissful to feel so relaxed and carefree. She couldn't remember the last time she'd felt this way and it was all due to a fabulous dinner, a place no one could find them, and Max and his care.

She followed him out past the tennis courts and the light of the moon reflected off the beaten dirt path in patches to illuminate their way.

Lush foliage closed in on the path but the moon made the leaves silvery and unthreatening. Somewhere she could hear water as it tinkled over rocks, and nocturnal animals scurried away from the intruders who had interrupted their night's business.

'So where are we going?' Georgia stumbled over a tree root that had bulged into the path and Max caught her wrist to steady her. His fingers sent warm trails up her arm and she felt cocooned in an aura of protection she didn't want to push away.

'Glow-Worm Gully is along this path called the Wishing Tree Track.' He squeezed her hand. 'You'll just have to hang onto me.'

'How fortunate you know where you're going.' She glanced up at him.

'Isn't it? This was my favourite treat when

Beatrice stayed here, although she complained all the way down and all the way back. I can remember much trivia from those times so watch out or I may inflict it on you.'

Georgia stumbled again. 'Don't normal people carry a torch?'

'Sorry.' Max slowed his pace. 'Yes, and I have one, but if I shine it on a glow-worm, it won't turn its light back on for fifteen minutes.'

'So we stumble along in the pitch black.'

He sighed loudly. 'It is not pitch black. It's called becoming accustomed to the dark.'

'Sheesh. It's like school again.' She could feel his smile even though she couldn't see it, which made the smile widen on her own face. 'So tell me about glow-worms. What is a fungus gnat?'

'A fungus gnat is a bit like a mosquito—hence the gnat part—and the larvae it lays are encased in bioluminescent cases that attract insects onto the sticky threads hanging below.'

'And if I was to ask the definition of bioluminescent?'

'It means luminous from chemical byproducts produced by the larvae. The blue-green glow from the larvae's taillight attracts the larvae's food.'

'So excretion? Poo light?'

'You are such a downer.'

'Realism, sunny boy. I'm a realist.'

'If you want realism, that's not all the glow-worms attract. They attract tourists—about six million dollars' worth for tour operators a year.'

The conversation stopped because they'd rounded a bend in the path and ahead and to the side, in the cracks and crevices under a deep overhang of rock, tiny tendrils of blue-green luminescence shone in hundreds of strands.

The more she looked, the more she saw. Georgia was silenced. Her hand tightened on Max's and she sighed with delight.

'Wow. Now, that's one spectacular show.'

She could tell Max was pleased with himself and her response.

'You should appreciate the world of the glow-worm,' he said. 'Every time a midge or similar insect runs into a hanging line it sticks and is hauled up by the worm, using its mouth, and stored for later.'

'So much for my fantasy of pretty glowing worms swinging in a friendly fashion in the dark.'

She frowned. 'In that case, they have a remarkable similarity to my ex-husband.'

She felt Max's scrutiny and he didn't say anything for a moment. Then he squeezed her hand again. 'Let's not spoil the night. Would you like to know about the mating habits of the parents?'

She appreciated his effort but she was upset with herself for destroying the mood.

Georgia slipped her hand out of his and rubbed her arms. It had been fun but now she just wanted to get back to Elsa. 'I don't think so. It was lovely, Max, but let's go back.'

Max got it. She could see that even in the semi-dark. 'Of course. Tomorrow we might come back and see the path by daylight. It is magnificent along here.'

'Sure.'

They returned to the guesthouse and Morgan's daughter was happy to see them. Elsa had woken up and in her less than discreet way had decided she wanted her mother.

By the time Georgia had calmed her daughter, Max had showered and reappeared in boxers and white T-shirt for bed.

Georgia tried not to look but the fabric stretched across his chest and biceps lovingly and activated somnolent nerves deep in her stomach. He looked far too masculine to easily ignore and she wasn't sure she was safer sharing a room with him at all.

'I'll take her if you want to change.' He held out his hands towards the baby and Elsa went happily to him.

For Georgia it felt as if she'd just handed over her only form of protection and she stepped back quickly.

Max frowned but didn't say anything as he turned away with Elsa and walked to the window. 'See the stars, Elsa? They're like glow-worms in the sky. Mummy saw the glow-worms tonight.'

Georgia could hear him talking away to Elsa as she closed the bathroom door. Now, why had she behaved like that? It wasn't as if Max was going to jump on her.

More likely she'd had the urge to run her hands

over him—though he did have a partiality to follow her lead when she made an offer—so it would be very easy to start something.

All through her shower, every touch of her own hand made her think of last night and of Max.

When she dried herself, even the towel seemed to sensitise her skin.

She was not going there. No matter what Max said or did she would not sleep with him. Absolutely. She chewed her lip as she opened the door.

When she came out of the bathroom Max had settled Elsa back in the cot, climbed into his own bed, and turned his bedside light out.

She guessed it was his way of saying she didn't have to worry. It was unfortunate that she felt lonely and frustrated when she climbed into her own generous bed and pulled up the thick duvet.

'Goodnight, Max,' she said, and she blushed in the dark at the forlorn note in her voice.

'Goodnight, Georgia.'

The next morning was fun.

After breakfast served in front of the fire Max carried Elsa in a pouch on his chest and they tramped along winding bush tracks and picnicked beside a mountain stream above a waterfall.

Elsa loved being with Max and Georgia wouldn't have minded it herself to be that close to Max's gorgeous chest. She was definitely becoming more fixated. Luckily the other scenery was spectacular as well.

When they arrived back at the retreat for afternoon tea, they were all exhausted but exhilarated from the mountain air. It was sad to have to pack to leave.

Max promised they would come again in the not-too-distant future, and Georgia added the day to her increasing store of wonderful memories with Max.

The phone call came just as Max carried Elsa to the car.

Georgia had gone back to the room for one last check that they hadn't left anything behind when the room phone rang.

She frowned and picked it up. 'Had a nice weekend, Mrs Winton?'

Sol! Nausea rose like a wave in her throat and she sucked the air in through her nostrils and swallowed before she could open her mouth.

Her voice when it came out was husky with distress. 'I'm not Mrs Winton!'

'No,' Sol said. 'You're Mrs Beresford—so I hear—but not for long! I'm coming for you and our daughter. But something needs to be done first.'

Then he rang off.

CHAPTER TEN

THE handset dropped from her fingers and spun giddily at the end of its cord beside the table. Georgia backed unsteadily across the room until she bumped into the bed behind her just as her legs collapsed from under her and she sat back limply. She hugged her knees.

How had Sol tracked her up here? She straightened slowly and looked around the room for inspiration. She had to tell Max he was in danger.

Then the next thought crashed into her. If she told Max, what would he do? She knew what he would do. He'd search out Sol—if Sol could find them then Max could find Sol—and Max had sworn he would not let Sol upset her again.

She needed to think this through before she talked to Max. He had to be safe. She heard his footsteps before he arrived and she tried to school her face.

'What are you doing?' Max stopped at the door and looked in. 'Elsa's in the car and Morgan is watching her. Are you ready to go?'

She didn't meet his eyes and something made him cross the room to sit beside her. 'Hello? You OK, sweetheart?'

Her eyes met his briefly but skidded away as if searching for something. 'I'm sorry, Max. I just had a really rotten pain in my head and it made me feel quite sick.'

Max frowned. He didn't like the sound of that. 'You're not going to have a cerebral aneurysm on me, are you?'

She forced a laugh. 'Typical doctor. Always assume the worst case scenario. Not anything as dramatic. I've a headache. Maybe even the beginnings of a migraine.'

She stood up and he saw that she was quite unsteady on her feet. He took her wrist and measured her pulse. Her heart rate was flying.

'Maybe we should stay here until you feel better. We can do that if you like.'

'No!' She'd answered too sharply and Max watched her try to play down her agitation and his gut tightened. 'Elsa's already in the car, you said. I'll be fine. It will be good to be home.'

Max studied her face. 'Are you all right, Georgia?'

'I'll be fine.' She turned towards the door and he could see she forced herself to take steps that she could barely manage. 'I'd really rather go home.'

At least she thought of it as home. 'All right.' Max put his hand under her elbow. 'Lean on me if you have to.'

Max tucked Georgia into the car and shut her door. He didn't like the way she looked and he would be happier when he had her home and settled.

He kissed Morgan's cheek. 'Thank you for making us so welcome.'

'You come back soon, Max. Your wife is a lovely woman.'

'Thanks, Morgan. I think so.'

Paddy came out from inside and wiped his hands on his trousers. 'Safe trip, friend.' He peered into the car and waved at Georgia. 'Your wife get the phone call from the other doctor, did she?'

Max stared at him and then nodded. He plastered a smile on his face when it was the last thing he felt like doing. 'Yes. Thanks.' They shook hands and Paddy and Morgan stood arm in arm to watch Max climb into the car.

Max kept smiling until they left the driveway. He didn't know what else to do. He glanced across at Georgia but she had her head back and her eyes closed.

Obviously Georgia had been in contact with Sol and she wasn't going to tell him.

That knowledge hit him like a hammer. It certainly explained the sudden headache and also his sudden urge to squeeze the life out of the defenceless steering-wheel beneath his fingers. He concentrated on loosening his grip without taking his eyes from the road.

If she didn't trust him then there wasn't much he could do except watch and wait.

But it was galling to think she wouldn't share her troubles with him. He'd thought them closer than that.

When they got home Georgia went straight to bed after feeding Elsa and Max watched her go. She'd said thanks for the weekend and nothing else and Max took his disappointment through to the library.

He'd do some background checks on Dr Winton, and he had a friend at Lower Mountains who owed him a favour.

Georgia knew that the sooner she distanced herself from Max the safer he would be. She needed to prepare a reason for her sudden disappearance and do as much as she could to safeguard Max's reputation. She needed to go to work one more day.

On Monday morning Karissa handed over the ward keys to Georgia. She turned back on her way out. 'By the way, I faxed a copy of the notes from your premature twins lady the other day. Some doctor wanted a copy of drugs given and not given. So if they ring, I've already done it.'

Georgia felt her stomach plummet. 'Did they say who wanted it?'

Karissa thought for a moment and then reached into the waste-paper basket and pulled out a screwed-up scrap of paper. She straightened it out. 'Yep. Didn't say why they wanted it but it was addressed to this guy. Dr S. Winton.'

It had started again. She'd known it would and yesterday's call had at least slightly prepared her.

The specialist's desire for Del to not have the treatment they'd expected became ominously clear. Sol had risked Del's twins' welfare to trap Max into not giving optimal care.

This was it, then. It was as if a blinding light flashed on in her head. The time for feeling sick and frightened had long passed and he was not going to win.

Now was time to put an end to this. She would not allow Sol to do this to Max. She, and anyone close to her, would not be a victim ever again.

She would leave this afternoon. Her mind was incredibly clear as she planned ahead.

'Before you go, Karissa. I need to let you know I can't do this week or next week after all. I'll be seeing the nurse manager today. My uncle is sick and I have to go back to Sydney. Max is staying here for the moment.'

Karissa sighed and then shrugged. 'I'm sorry about your uncle. Hope he's OK.'

Georgia could answer that honestly. 'He's been like a father to me since my parents died. I won't know how sick he is until I get there.

'In a few months I might even be looking at coming back up this way so I will try to get a few weeks together to help you get away.'

'Bummer you're leaving.' Then Karissa smiled philosophically. 'I hadn't booked anything yet in case it didn't work out. No worries. I can wait or something will come along.'

'I'm so sorry to have to let you down.'

Karissa shrugged. 'Maybe we'll catch you again.' She gave Georgia a hug. 'Never mind. Hope your uncle improves. It's been nice meeting you.'

Georgia watched her go and told herself she hadn't lied. Harry was sick. And if she didn't do something about Sol for once and for all, her life would continue to be a series of abrupt departures.

The time had come and she wasn't even afraid any more. Just incredibly, volcanically angry. How dared he?

For the moment all she knew was that she would never go back to Sol but she just as surely couldn't stay with Max. When she left Max, Sol had better leave him alone—or else.

Tayla's wedding plans would keep Tayla out of her way and Uncle Harry would have no problem with Elsa and herself moving into his house while she planned Sol's downfall.

If she told Max why she was going, he would want to take Sol on and save the world for her. But this was something she had to do for herself and for Elsa.

She would not allow Max to be dragged though the type of mud-slinging investigation Sol would have in mind. It was all her fault and it was time that she stopped being a victim.

The last thing she wanted was for Max to go

after Sol so she'd have to leave without telling him. Georgia looked down at her mobile phone. She'd have to turn it off or Max would phone her and she knew she would cry.

CHAPTER ELEVEN

GEORGIA was gone.

She'd hired a car and left with Elsa as if there had been nothing between them.

Mrs White was devastated and the house had felt like a morgue without Georgia and Elsa when he'd come home from work. Now her phone was switched off.

Max knew Georgia had left because of Winton but how could she respect *him* so little that she hadn't even told him her ex-husband had contacted her. Or even that she was going?

What did she want him to think and why? Why not tell the truth?

Max stared out over the ocean and thought about all the possible reasons she had felt unable to talk to him. The most obvious one fell into place with a dull, ominous thud.

How had Winton got her back last time? Max slapped the veranda rail. With a threat to her friend! What if this time he'd threatened not Georgia or Elsa, but *him*?

Max glared out to sea and his hand tightened on the veranda rail. He wasn't worried about any threat Sol Winton could make to him but he was livid that Georgia had felt so powerless that she'd left to protect him.

Her lack of faith in his ability to protect himself, or her, hurt the most.

She had no idea of the cut-throat world of hospital administration, then, he thought, and smiled without humour.

It was his job to sort out troublemakers and those with plans for self-gain. He dealt with mini-gods like Winton all the time.

That would explain why Georgia hadn't told him about the phone call if she was concerned he would take matters into his own hands.

He had to find Winton, disarm him once and for all, with a cast-iron insurance against any further threats. Then he, Georgia and Elsa could get on with their lives together.

After that he would find Georgia and tell her he loved her.

Enough of this pussyfooting around. He wanted his family. She'd be with Harry. It was the logical place for her to go.

He rang the retired doctor from Meeandah who agreed to come back on call for the next two days while Max was away.

Then he offered Mrs White leave if she wanted it but she said she'd prefer to stay in case Georgia came back.

He threw some overnight clothes in his case and after one last phone call to his friend at Lower Mountains he climbed into his vehicle. Sol's plan had been quashed and an investigation started. The paper trail would catch Winton in the end and Max had made sure he would be drummed out of the medical fraternity.

When Max pulled out into the highway traffic the headlights of a truck coming straight for him made him swerve violently towards the side of the mountain.

Normally it would have been easy to correct the swerve. This time when he applied the brakes the pedal sank uselessly to the floor.

His last thought as the Hummer crashed through the guide rail was that he'd underestimated Sol, but at least he was in a decent vehicle for the hurtle down the mountainside.

Georgia's hand shook as she dialled Sol's home number. Elsa was finally asleep and cars whizzed past the motor inn she'd stopped at for the night.

She hadn't wanted to land on Harry's doorstep at midnight but she needed to let Sol know she had left Max and hopefully forestall any plans Sol had to cause trouble.

The phone rang six times and with each ring Georgia could feel her heart rate increase. Her mouth dried and suddenly she realised how emotionally fragile she was—and playing into Sol's hands. She put the phone down and stared at her fingers on the handset.

What was she doing? Hadn't she learned that weakness and not being prepared for confrontation with Sol caused more problems? She needed to be much smarter this time. It wasn't just herself at stake.

She needed proof that Sol was unbalanced and that he intended to threaten and blackmail her into submission again. She needed to ensure Sol could never take Elsa.

She would buy herself a tiny tape recorder to wear on her person. Then she would take the proof to the police and formally charge him. She should have done that a long time ago and she owed it to Max and herself to do it now.

Max's faith in her stood clear and firm and she knew she would do it this time. She would do this and then she would find Max and tell him she loved him.

The next morning, she and Elsa set things in motion. This time she would ensure she was safe.

She tucked the tiny voice-activated tape recorder inside her shirt and patted the small cylinder in her jacket pocket. The final purchase had been a last-minute decision and one that provided reassuring support.

She glanced in the rear-view mirror at her sleeping daughter. It was time to set up a meeting with Sol somewhere safe, like a public park.

She watched Elsa in the car outside the phone booth. Her daughter slept on as she dialled Sol's office.

'Dr Winton has gone away on urgent family business.' Sol's secretary's comment sounded as though it had been repeated many times. 'He won't be back until Wednesday.'

'Thank you.' Georgia put down the phone and returned to the car. She looked at Elsa. 'Now, that's an anticlimax, Elsa. I wonder where he went?'

Suddenly Georgia's heart rate picked up. Georgia snatched the mobile phone from her bag and checked the missed calls.

They'd flooded in. One from Max, one from Sol, four from Max's house at Byron Bay.

She stared at the calls and shuddered. Then the phone vibrated in her hand and she checked the number. Private.

She looked back at Elsa, drew a deep breath and pressed the button.

'Hello?'

'Georgia Beresford?' She didn't recognise the voice and her shoulders dropped in relief that it wasn't Sol.

'Yes?'

'Constable Ethan Moss, Byron Police Station.'

Georgia's heart thumped so loudly in her ears she could barely hear the man. She forced words out. 'Is something wrong?'

'We've been trying to contact you. Do you have a husband by the name of Max Beresford?'

Oh, no, please, God, she thought. 'Yes I do.'

'I'm sorry to have to tell you your husband was involved in a vehicle accident on the Pacific Highway last night and was airlifted in a critical condition to Newcastle Hospital.'

In slow motion she took the phone from her ear and looked at it. This couldn't be happening. She put the phone back to her ear and her hand was shaking. 'Is Max going to be all right?'

The voice was sympathetic but pragmatic. 'I suggest you ask his doctors that question, Mrs Beresford.'

'I will. Newcastle, you said.'

'That is correct, madam. His vehicle was destroyed in the descent but managed to protect him enough for the rescue crews to be able to transfer him to hospital alive.'

'Thank you.'

'Good morning, Mrs Beresford.'

Georgia dropped the phone on the seat beside her and lowered her head onto the steering-wheel.

Max. In an accident and critical. For a moment she couldn't think of the direction she needed to take to head north. She didn't know where to start.

Sol's whereabouts were the last thing she had to worry about now. She needed to get to Max.

Her phone rang again and she snatched it off the seat. 'Yes?'

'Mrs Beresford?'

'Mrs White?'

There was a pause then, 'Thank God I've been

able to contact you.' Georgia could hear the tears in Mrs White's voice and her own throat closed. 'The doctor is dangerously ill.'

Georgia tried to keep her own voice steady. 'I know. The police just rang me. I'm in Sydney but will drive to Newcastle as soon as I hang up.'

'I'm at the hospital but he's still in Theatre. Has been all night. They won't give me any information because I'm not the next of kin.'

Poor Mrs White. She loved Max like a son. 'I'll be there in an hour. We'll wait together with Elsa. Did you drive down last night?'

'They rang for you at eight and I left soon after that when I couldn't get you on the phone. I thought you would go to the hospital as soon as you heard and would need me there.'

'Thank you, Mrs White. It's good to know I have someone to share the waiting with. I'll see you soon.' Georgia ended the call and put the phone down.

She looked at Elsa strapped in the back and started the car. She concentrated resolutely on her driving. She couldn't allow negative thoughts to take her concentration. Max needed them to get there safely.

Deep down, inside her, along with the ball of fear in case she was too late, she knew that Max needed her.

When Georgia arrived at Newcastle Hospital she was directed to a waiting room outside the intensive care unit. Mrs White was there with mascara-stained tissues spread around her.

'I'd been trying to ring you all night since they rang me.' Mrs White's big panda eyes were smeared from crying.

'I know. I'm sorry.' Georgia gave her a hug and Mrs White hugged her back.

'How is he?'

'He came out of Theatre about half an hour ago and they took him straight into Intensive Care. I said you would be here soon and they said to ring the bell as soon as you arrived.'

Georgia took a deep breath and stepped across to the door to push the bell. 'I'll take the baby.' Mrs White held out her hands and Elsa glared at her mother as she was handed over.

'Mummy will be back soon,' Mrs White said to Elsa. 'She needs to make sure Daddy is all right.'

Georgia heard the housekeeper's words as she opened the door and tears stung her eyes. Mrs White was right. Max was Elsa's daddy in all the important ways and she vowed that if Max made it they would be the family she had come to realise they had both always wanted.

Stepping into Intensive Care was like stepping into a nightmare.

Georgia knew what the equipment did, she knew the sounds and smells, but she'd never had someone she loved totally dependent on the machines and personnel in this unit.

'I'm Mrs Beresford. I'd like to see my husband,

Max, please. I understand he has just come out of Theatre.'

The intensive care nurse nodded sympathetically. 'I'll just get the registrar to see you before you go in, Mrs Beresford.'

The registrar was tall and gangly and he looked far too young to be in charge of Max's survival.

'I'm Dr Blaxland, Mrs Beresford. This all must be a horrible shock for you. It is for us, too. Max is well liked and respected in this hospital and we will do everything we can.'

He may have looked young but intelligence shone from his eyes, along with warm empathy, and Georgia revised her opinion.

'How is he?' Georgia didn't like the sound of 'everything we can'. 'I understand he is lucky to be alive.'

'He's been in Theatre most of the night. The surgeons had problems with severe internal bleeding as well as a blow to the head. Luckily there doesn't seem to be any spinal involvement.'

'He will live?'

'Dr Beresford has a tenacious hold on life and is breathing for himself, yes. He's critical but stable at the moment. Our main concern is his lack of consciousness since his return from Theatre but cerebral oedema would account for that and hopefully will resolve over the next few hours or days. Thankfully the CAT scan doesn't show any cerebral bleeding.'

Georgia couldn't take it all in because she needed to see for herself that Max was alive. 'Can I see him?'

'Of course. This way.'

Dr Blaxland showed Georgia into a single room. When Georgia first saw Max it was hard to see the man she loved beneath all the equipment. The blinds were drawn so it was dim but the beeping of the cardiac monitor proved that Max was alive. Thank God.

A young nurse stood up from the chair beside the bed and Dr Blaxland introduced her. 'This is Ellie. She's one of our brightest stars in ICU. Your husband is in good hands.'

'Mrs Beresford.' Ellie smiled and indicated for Georgia to take the chair she had vacated. 'He's not responding at the moment but that doesn't mean he can't hear your voice. I'll just step outside for a moment to give you privacy but I'll be watching the monitors at the desk.'

'Thank you, Ellie. And for your care of Max.'

'Dr Beresford was very good to me when I did my obstetric rotation in my training. It's a privilege.'

The young woman left and Georgia sat down.

She picked up Max's hand and pressed it to her cheek, careful not to entangle any of the intravenous lines. He felt warm and that in itself was reassuring.

'Oh, Max. Why didn't I tell you I loved you when I had the chance?'

The heart-rate monitor continued its steady beat and she could see the gentle rise and fall of his chest. He was alive and there was hope.

Lots of hope.

Max was going to make it and they would start again.

In the face of this Sol was nothing, and somehow she knew he would never be a problem again.

Georgia stayed with Max for an hour and then she left to allow Mrs White to go in.

Sitting in the waiting room with a sleeping Elsa beside her on the lounge, Georgia could do nothing but stare at the walls.

She remembered the tape recorder in her shirt and pulled it out. She'd left it on by mistake. Voice activated, it had recorded what she had to say to Max. She sat and listened to the doctor's words again.

When she came to the part where she told Max that she loved him the tears flowed down her cheeks and she turned the playback off and slid it back into her pocket to put it away.

The man at the door paused as he saw her. Slowly he smiled. 'Don't cry. I'm still here for you.'

Georgia turned her head slowly and her eyes narrowed. Sol. Here. The last place he was wanted.

How had he known?

Her fingers curled into fists and she felt for the recorder and activated record.

'What are you doing here, Sol?'

'I've come to claim what is rightfully mine. To bring you and my daughter home.'

Suddenly it all became clear that she had been the one who had allowed Sol's control over her to continue. From this moment and this place it would never happen again. Not in a million years.

'Go away, Sol.'

'I'm not leaving.' He was so confident. She could see it in his conceited face. He was a despicable bully and a fool and finally she was immune.

She stood up and faced him and all the love she held for Max rose inside her like the walls of a fortress.

'I'm not afraid of you any more, Sol.' She raised her chin and cold contempt dripped from her voice.

'The man I love is in a critical condition through those doors and if I find out that you have done anything to harm him I will take you and your high-profile job apart piece by piece.'

Sol raised his eyebrows and shrugged. 'I don't know what you mean.'

Georgia's eyes narrowed. 'I remember when you threatened to discredit Denise at Lower Mountains. I know you have acquired papers to attempt something similar to Max at Meeandah.'

He smiled down at her and then at the sleeping Elsa and Georgia's skin crawled with contempt. She felt like snatching Elsa up and walking away but she wanted him properly hung and this was her chance.

Sol went on conversationally. 'If you and our daughter come with me, he'll be safe.'

'What are you saying and what are you planning, Sol?'

He smirked. 'Just a little medication review. But

if he doesn't wake up, that won't be necessary.' It was as she'd thought. Then his last words sank in.

'What do you know about Max's accident?'

He shook his head but he couldn't help his smile. 'Had a little brake problem with his fabulous Hummer, did he?'

Georgia felt the nausea rise in her throat and her hand tightened over the can of mace in her pocket.

Her voice hardened to steel and she felt as though she were ten times his size.

Small, insignificant, despicable little man that he was. 'Leave now, Sol, and be very, very frightened. Because I am going to drum you out of this country, if not into gaol, and you will never work again. I should have done it a year ago but I will do it now. I have the proof and I will use it.'

She smiled at him through her teeth. 'Don't ever come near myself or my daughter or anyone in my family again.'

He took a step back from the implacability in her face and she stared him down.

'Get out.' She said it with finality and he went.

When he left there was no jaunty spring in his step and she forgot him as soon as he was out of her sight because Mrs White had returned.

She didn't see the policeman step up to him and take his arm and march him away. She had other more important things to worry about.

'They said for you to come back in.' Mrs White looked down at Elsa who woke up as the door shut with a clang. She bent to lift Elsa but Georgia stayed her arm.

'I'll take Elsa in to her daddy this time.'

Mrs White bit her lip and nodded.

'I'll be back soon,' Georgia said, and pushed open the doors with her daughter in her arms.

'You're not supposed to bring children in here,' Ellie said quietly, but she didn't try to stop Georgia.

Georgia smiled. 'I know. But I want Elsa to see her father for a few minutes and then I'll take her out.'

'That's fine. I'll be just outside.'

Georgia sat down in the chair with Elsa on her lap and Elsa crowed when she saw Max.

'Yes, darling. Here's your daddy and when he is well, we will all go home together.'

Tears stung her eyes. Max had to get better. Elsa needed her dad and she needed her man.

'My past is over, Max. Sol can't frighten me any more. He will never intrude on us again and I need you to wake up so we can start our lives together.

'Elsa needs her daddy and I need the man I love to come back to me. I want to deliver babies with you. I want to be a grandparent with you when Elsa grows up. Please, Max. I love you so much.'

Max's eyelids flickered and Georgia held her breath.

His tongue moved to moisten his lips and she lifted his hand again and kissed it. 'I'm here, Max, darling. Elsa and I are both here. We love you, Max, and you need to get better to be with us.'

Max opened his eyes and stared at the woman he loved. She was here and she'd said she loved him. His gaze travelled to the baby girl frowning fiercely at him and his lips twitched in a smile.

'Hello, family,' he said croakily, and went back to sleep.

CHAPTER TWELVE

THREE months later the chapel floated like a snow-flake against the backdrop of the lush Hunter Valley Gardens and an old-fashioned organ, not a string quartet, delivered soaring notes out over the waiting guests.

Max Beresford stood tall and straight at the front of the church and knew without doubt he was doing the right thing.

Winton had been charged with attempted murder and Georgia's recording made at the hospital had helped convict her ex-husband, along with the testimony of more people than they'd realised he'd affected, and the results of Max's own investigations.

Winton had signed adoption papers and Georgia and Elsa were safe—just as Max had promised in the beginning—but now it was a new beginning.

When Georgia, the woman who had been his wife but never his bride, paused at the door of the church, Max's heart swelled with the music and everything else left his mind except the fact that this woman would share his destiny for ever.

Georgia looked radiant in a long simple cream dress with the tiniest cream veil holding back her glorious hair. This time was for real and he smiled at the tiny feather she'd tucked into her veil to tease him.

Georgia walked slowly but confidently towards him on her uncle's arm and her eyes shone with the love he'd been humbled to realise was truly his.

When he took Georgia's hand he cradled her fingers against his cheek for a moment and she smiled shyly up at him.

'Hello my bride.'

'Hello, Max.'

They both looked across the congregation to Elsa, who glared at them both from Mrs White's arms. Georgia shook her head at Elsa's quivering lip.

Max glanced at the minister and said something quietly to the man then held out his arms. Mrs White brought the little girl across and Max tucked her onto his hip before they proceeded.

He smiled down at Georgia. 'She should be here with us,' Max said. 'After all, she introduced us.'

0308 Gen Std HB

APRIL 2008 HARDBACK TITLES

ROMANCE

The Sheikh's Blackmailed Mistress *Penny Jordan*	978 0 263 20270 0
The Millionaire's Inexperienced Love-Slave *Miranda Lee*	978 0 263 20271 7
Bought: The Greek's Innocent Virgin *Sarah Morgan*	978 0 263 20272 4
Bedded at the Billionaire's Convenience *Cathy Williams*	978 0 263 20273 1
The Billionaire Boss's Secretary Bride *Helen Brooks*	978 0 263 20274 8
The Giannakis Bride *Catherine Spencer*	978 0 263 20275 5
Desert King, Pregnant Mistress *Susan Stephens*	978 0 263 20276 2
Ruthless Boss, Hired Wife *Kate Hewitt*	978 0 263 20277 9
The Pregnancy Promise *Barbara McMahon*	978 0 263 20278 6
The Italian's Cinderella Bride *Lucy Gordon*	978 0 263 20279 3
Saying Yes to the Millionaire *Fiona Harper*	978 0 263 20280 9
Her Royal Wedding Wish *Cara Colter*	978 0 263 20281 6
SOS Marry Me! *Melissa McClone*	978 0 263 20282 3
Her Baby, His Proposal *Teresa Carpenter*	978 0 263 20283 0
Marrying the Runaway Bride *Jennifer Taylor*	978 0 263 20284 7
The Fatherhood Miracle *Margaret Barker*	978 0 263 20285 4

HISTORICAL

Untouched Mistress *Margaret McPhee*	978 0 263 20195 6
A Less Than Perfect Lady *Elizabeth Beacon*	978 0 263 20196 3
Viking Warrior, Unwilling Wife *Michelle Styles*	978 0 263 20197 0

MEDICAL™

Single Dad Seeks a Wife *Melanie Milburne*	978 0 263 19890 4
Her Four Year Baby Secret *Alison Roberts*	978 0 263 19891 1
Country Doctor, Spring Bride *Abigail Gordon*	978 0 263 19892 8
The Midwife's Baby *Fiona McArthur*	978 0 263 19893 5

0308 Gén Std LP

Pure reading pleasure

APRIL 2008 LARGE PRINT TITLES

ROMANCE

The Desert Sheikh's Captive Wife *Lynne Graham*	978 0 263 20034 8
His Christmas Bride *Helen Brooks*	978 0 263 20035 5
The Demetrios Bridal Bargain *Kim Lawrence*	978 0 263 20036 2
The Spanish Prince's Virgin Bride *Sandra Marton*	978 0 263 20037 9
The Millionaire Tycoon's English Rose *Lucy Gordon*	978 0 263 20038 6
Snowbound with Mr Right *Judy Christenberry*	978 0 263 20039 3
The Boss's Little Miracle *Barbara McMahon*	978 0 263 20040 9
His Christmas Angel *Michelle Douglas*	978 0 263 20041 6

HISTORICAL

Housemaid Heiress *Elizabeth Beacon*	978 0 263 20145 1
Marrying Captain Jack *Anne Herries*	978 0 263 20149 9
My Lord Footman *Claire Thornton*	978 0 263 20153 6

MEDICAL™

The Italian Count's Baby *Amy Andrews*	978 0 263 19944 4
The Nurse He's Been Waiting For *Meredith Webber*	978 0 263 19945 1
His Long-Awaited Bride *Jessica Matthews*	978 0 263 19946 8
A Woman To Belong To *Fiona Lowe*	978 0 263 19947 5
Wedding at Pelican Beach *Emily Forbes*	978 0 263 19948 2
Dr Campbell's Secret Son *Anne Fraser*	978 0 263 19949 9

0408 Gen Std HB

MAY 2008 HARDBACK TITLES

ROMANCE

Bought for Revenge, Bedded for Pleasure	978 0 263 20286 1
Emma Darcy	
Forbidden: The Billionaire's Virgin Princess	978 0 263 20287 8
Lucy Monroe	
The Greek Tycoon's Convenient Wife	978 0 263 20288 5
Sharon Kendrick	
The Marciano Love-Child *Melanie Milburne*	978 0 263 20289 2
The Millionaire's Rebellious Mistress	978 0 263 20290 8
Catherine George	
The Mediterranean Billionaire's Blackmail Bargain	
Abby Green	978 0 263 20291 5
Mistress Against Her Will *Lee Wilkinson*	978 0 263 20292 2
Her Ruthless Italian Boss *Christina Hollis*	978 0 263 20293 9
Parents in Training *Barbara McMahon*	978 0 263 20294 6
Newlyweds of Convenience *Jessica Hart*	978 0 263 20295 3
The Desert Prince's Proposal *Nicola Marsh*	978 0 263 20296 0
Adopted: Outback Baby *Barbara Hannay*	978 0 263 20297 7
Winning the Single Mum's Heart	978 0 263 20298 4
Linda Goodnight	
Boardroom Bride and Groom *Shirley Jump*	978 0 263 20299 1
Proposing to the Children's Doctor	978 0 263 20300 4
Joanna Neil	
Emergency: Wife Needed *Emily Forbes*	978 0 263 20301 1

HISTORICAL

The Virtuous Courtesan *Mary Brendan*	978 0 263 20198 7
The Homeless Heiress *Anne Herries*	978 0 263 20199 4
Rebel Lady, Convenient Wife *June Francis*	978 0 263 20200 7

MEDICAL™

Virgin Midwife, Playboy Doctor	978 0 263 19894 2
Margaret McDonagh	
The Rebel Doctor's Bride *Sarah Morgan*	978 0 263 19895 9
The Surgeon's Secret Baby Wish *Laura Iding*	978 0 263 19896 6
Italian Doctor, Full-time Father *Dianne Drake*	978 0 263 19897 3

0408 Gen Std LP

Pure reading pleasure

MAY 2008 LARGE PRINT TITLES

ROMANCE

The Italian Billionaire's Ruthless Revenge *Jacqueline Baird*	978 0 263 20042 3
Accidentally Pregnant, Conveniently Wed *Sharon Kendrick*	978 0 263 20043 0
The Sheikh's Chosen Queen *Jane Porter*	978 0 263 20044 7
The Frenchman's Marriage Demand *Chantelle Shaw*	978 0 263 20045 4
Her Hand in Marriage *Jessica Steele*	978 0 263 20046 1
The Sheikh's Unsuitable Bride *Liz Fielding*	978 0 263 20047 8
The Bridesmaid's Best Man *Barbara Hannay*	978 0 263 20048 5
A Mother in a Million *Melissa James*	978 0 263 20049 2

HISTORICAL

The Vanishing Viscountess *Diane Gaston*	978 0 263 20154 3
A Wicked Liaison *Christine Merrill*	978 0 263 20155 0
Virgin Slave, Barbarian King *Louise Allen*	978 0 263 20156 7

MEDICAL™

The Magic of Christmas *Sarah Morgan*	978 0 263 19950 5
Their Lost-and-Found Family *Marion Lennox*	978 0 263 19951 2
Christmas Bride-To-Be *Alison Roberts*	978 0 263 19952 9
His Christmas Proposal *Lucy Clark*	978 0 263 19953 6
Baby: Found at Christmas *Laura Iding*	978 0 263 19954 3
The Doctor's Pregnancy Bombshell *Janice Lynn*	978 0 263 19955 0